GUNSMOKE TRAIL

GUNSMOKE TRAIL

Jackson Cole

This Large Print book is published by BBC Audiobooks Ltd, Bath, England and by Thorndike Press®, Waterville, Maine, USA.

Published in 2006 in the U.K. by arrangement with Golden West Literary Agency.

Published in 2006 in the U.S. by arrangement with Golden West Literary Agency.

U.K. Hardcover   ISBN 1–4056–3798–6 (Chivers Large Print)
ISBN 13: 978 1 405 63798 5
U.K. Softcover   ISBN 1–4056–3799–4 (Camden Large Print)
ISBN 13: 978 1 405 63799 2
U.S. Softcover   ISBN 0–7862–8730–6 (British Favorites)

The text of this Large Print edition is unabridged.
Other aspects of the book may vary from the original edition.

Set in 16 pt. New Times Roman.

Printed in Great Britain on acid-free paper.

British Library Cataloguing in Publication Data available

Library of Congress Cataloging-in-Publication Data

Cole, Jackson.
    Gunsmoke trail / by Jackson Cole.
       p.   cm.
    "A Jim Hatfield western"—T.p. verso.
    ISBN 0–7862–8730–6 (pbk. : alk. paper)
    1. Hatfield, Jim (Fictitious character)—Fiction. 2. Texas Rangers—Fiction. 3. Outlaws—Fiction. 4. Texas—Fiction. 5. Large type books. I. Title.
PS3505.O2685G867 2006
813'.52—dc22   2006010231

CHAPTER ONE

'Goldy, if we can just manage to make it to the top of this infernal sag, I've a notion we'll find the Chihuahua Trail on the other side of it,' Jim Hatfield told his tall golden sorrel.

Goldy's answer was an explosive snort, and if horses can swear, that snort was undoubtedly a cuss word. The trail he was following was enough to make any horse swear. It was little more than a goat track slithering and squirming up a steep rise like a snake with the hiccups. Loose stones littered its surface, on which his irons slipped and skated, and there were holes in which it was easy to break a leg. But he was agile as a burro and his mighty strength surmounted the difficulties of the going.

Nevertheless, Goldy was gasping for breath when they finally reached the crest, a regular knife-edged hogback not more than fifty feet in width, with its far slope tumbling downward for several hundred yards and ending at a broad roadway that glimmered whitely in the moonlight.

'Yep, there she is,' Hatfield said, pulling the horse to a halt on the lip of the slope. 'There's the trail by way of which the carts and wagons come up from Mexico. That town of Aguilar we're headed for should be only a few miles to the south of here. You just take it easy and catch your wind while I have a smoke.'

Hooking one leg comfortably over the horn, he fished out the makin's and deftly rolled a cigarette with the slim fingers of his left hand.

Hatfield made a striking picture as he sat atop his great golden horse, the still flood of the moonlight outlining every detail of his sternly handsome face and rugged form. Very tall, much more than six feet, his broad shoulders and deep chest were in keeping with his height. He wore the simple but colorful garb of the rangeland—faded blue shirt and overalls, bat-wing chaps, high-heeled half-boots of softly tanned leather, broad-brimmed 'J.B.' A scarlet neckerchief was looped about his sinewy throat. His lean waist was encircled by double cartridge belts. From the carefully worked and oiled cut-out holsters protruded the plain black butts of heavy guns.

His face, with its lean, powerful jaw and chin, its rather wide mouth that grin-quirked at the corners, and its deeply bronzed cheeks and high-bridged nose, was dominated by black-lashed eyes of a peculiar shade of green.

As he smoked, Hatfield studied the broad gray ribbon of the old, old trail that rolls its travelled length from Chihuahua City in Mexico to San Antonio, Texas.

It was old, he knew, when the Spaniards first set foot upon it. Old when the Aztecs swarmed south to take over the land they named Anahuac. Old when the people who preceded the Aztecs established themselves in Mexico. Hatfield could imagine furtive, hairy figures on crooked-boned legs padding its surface in eerie silence under an orbed moon—the people of the early earth who left their strange relics and outlandish drawings in the caves of the Big Bend country. And even then, doubtless, the trail was old, for it is and always was the road from the fertile South across the arid lands to the grassy plains and silver streams of Texas. Smugglers, rustlers and marauding Mexicans used it in years gone by, and used it still. On its dusty expanse anything could happen, and usually did. The Gunsmoke Trail!

To the west were the Chianti Mountains, blue-black shadows against the starry filigree of the sky, to the east the Cienagas. To the south the distant waters of the Rio Grande and the crossing at Presidio, with the Mexican town of Ojinaga on the far bank of the Great River.

Hatfield pinched out his cigarette and settled himself in the saddle. 'Let's go, feller,' he said and rode down the slope, turning south when he reached the trail.

For a mile or more he rode swiftly, Goldy covering the smooth surface with long, effortless strides. They topped a low rise and Hatfield abruptly slowed the sorrel to a walk. Some two miles to the south he saw some dark blotches crawling along the trail. Pacing his horse slowly, in the shadow of a bristle of growth that shut off the moonlight, he studied the moving objects.

'Must be one of the cart trains heading north from Aguilar and bound for Sanders,' he mused. 'But what the devil is that over to the left?'

Sweeping out of the east, on a long slant that would eventually bring them to the trail, was a troop of six or seven hard-riding horsemen. Hatfield pulled Goldy to a halt.

'Chances are it's just a bunch of cowhands heading for town,' he muttered, 'but funny things been happening in this section lately. If they're really bound for the *pueblo* they'll hit the trail behind the cart train unless they alter their course. We'll just stay here out of sight, horse, till we see which way they turn.'

His eyes narrowed with interest as he noted that the riders were veering more and more to the west. A short straggle of growth that flanked the trail less than a mile to the south hid them from view. Hatfield waited for their reappearance, but as the minutes dragged past, there was no sign of movement save on the trail where the string of carts crawled slowly out of the south.

'Goldy, blamed if I don't believe those fast riding jiggers are holed up in that patch of brush!' he exclaimed suddenly. 'I wonder why. Begins to look like they're waiting for that cart train to come up with them. If they are, I'm willing to bet they're not just figuring on passing the time of day. This will stand a mite of investigating, if we can do it without getting our hides punctured.'

He studied the terrain ahead. To the left was a string of thickets a little distance back from the trail. If he could get behind them unnoticed, he could circle into the straggle of brush behind which the mysterious riders would be holed up at the edge of the trail if they actually had designs on the approaching cart train. He rode back down the rise a little way and then chanced riding out onto the moon-drenched prairie. Nothing happened and he continued until he was behind the first of the thickets. Then he turned Goldy's nose due south and rode parallel to the trail and some five hundred yards to the left.

The sorrel's irons made only a whisper of sound on the tall and heavy grass. Everything was easy until he reached the southerly edge of the thicket. Then there was an open space of about a hundred yards to cross. That was ticklish business. If the men in the brush—and Hatfield was convinced now that they were waiting for the cart train—had thought to post somebody to watch their back trail, the results might be decidedly unpleasant; it gave him a crawly feeling along his backbone to think of it.

The bright open space seemed very wide

indeed, out of proportion to the actual distance. Hatfield suspiciously noted how the moonbeams glinting on the leaves of the approaching thicket seemed to endow them with movement, as if they were being pressed gently aside by stealthy hands; how a patch of mica on a little bare spot glittered like malevolent eyes; how the shadows at the base of the growth appeared to crawl and writhe with sinister purpose. As he gained the shelter of the next thicket he abruptly realized that he had been holding his breath for the past minute. He hoped Goldy hadn't also, for if he had, he'd exhale it with an explosive snort that would carry a long way in the deathly still night. Apparently Goldy hadn't felt the fear that disturbed his rider, for he didn't snort.

The next open space was even worse. Hatfield was almost opposite the spot where he thought the bunch was holed up. Again he breathed deep relief when he gained the shelter of the third patch of mesquite and pulled Goldy to a walk. He brought him to a full stop at the far edge of the thicket and sat peering and listening. To his ears came the creak and rumble of the heavily laden carts that were now drawing near. Still not the slightest sound arose from the ominous straggle of brush edging the trail. Hatfield's black brows drew together; the lead cart must be almost opposite the place where the night riders had disappeared.

And then all hell broke loose at the edge of the trail. There was a roar of gunfire, shouts, screams, curses and cries of warning. The carts clashed to a halt as the mules that drew them milled in wild confusion. There were crashes as several vehicles were overturned by cramped wheels as the frenzied mules sought to escape the terror raging around them. A flare of reddish light ballooned up above the growth.

Hatfield's voice rang out—no need for silence any longer. 'Trail, Goldy, trail!'

'Trail, Goldy, trail!'

The great sorrel shot forward, his steely legs working like pistons, his irons drumming the ground. At a dead run Hatfield sent him flashing across the quarter of a mile of open prairie. The pandemonium increased as they neared the belt of growth.

They crashed into the brush and tore through it, heedless of thorns and branches. They burst through a final fringe of growth and onto a scene of wildest confusion. A few yards down the trail half a dozen men crouched in the edge of the growth and blazed away at the demoralized carters who were shooting wildly in return. One of the overturned carts had been fired and was burning fiercely. Lunging mules and screeching wheels added to the bedlam. Several dark forms lay motionless in the dust. The raid had been well staged and had taken the carters completely by surprise.

Hatfield jerked Goldy to a sliding halt, dropped the split reins and his hands streaked with lightning speed to his holsters. An instant later both his guns let go with a rattling crash. A howl of pain and cries of alarm answered the reports. The raiders whirled to face the attack, guns flaming. Hatfield felt the wind of passing bullets. One slashed a hole in his shirt sleeve. Another turned his hat sideways on his head. His big Colts bucked in his hands, their muzzles spouting flame and smoke. He saw one of the raiders pitch forward on his face. Another reeled sideways to lie in a crumpled heap. Hatfield heard the hammers of his guns click on spent shells. He slammed the empty sixes into their sheaths and jerked his heavy Winchester from the saddle boot.

With Goldy doing a weird, elusive dance that made him a most difficult target, Hatfield threw down with the saddle gun, then abruptly realized there was nothing to shoot at. The raiders had dived into the shelter of the brush. As he started to spray the growth with lead, he heard a prodigious crashing and a drumming of fast hoofs. The drygulchers were going away from there, fast. Hatfield whirled Goldy in pursuit and slammed squarely into a frantic mule that had broken away from a cart. Down went the mule, and down went Goldy on top of him. Hatfield barely had time to kick his feet free from the stirrups and hurl himself sideways. He hit the ground with stunning force and rolled over and over to escape the slashing hoofs of mule and horse. Goldy regained his footing and ran a little ways and stopped, blowing and snorting. The mule also scrambled off the ground and ran into the brush, braying like the trumpet of doom. The hoof beats of the fleeing raiders faded into the distance.

Hatfield started to rise, then flattened out on the ground. The carters were still firing wildly in every direction but the right one. He heard bullets clip the leaves over his head.

'Amigo!' He yelled at the top of his voice. 'Stop that blamed shooting! Amigo, I tell you, Amigo!' He repeated the command in Spanish.

The firing stopped. Hatfield got to his feet, a bit unsteadily, and strode forward into the circle of light cast by the blazing cart. The bewildered carters stood tense and ready, fingers on the triggers of their cocked guns.

'Get those carts moving!' Hatfield roared at them. 'Do you want the whole train to go up in smoke? Move!'

The voice of authority shook together some of their scattered senses. Cursing and muttering, they dived into the mess. Working like demons they got the mules under control and moved away from the blazing cart that was threatening to set fire to the others. Something like order was restored.

Hatfield reloaded his guns, retrieved his fallen Winchester and strode forward. A tall young Mexican came to meet him.

'Senor,' he said courteously, 'I know not who you are, but you arrived most timely. You delivered us from the mercy of those *ladrones* who know no mercy. *Gracias,* Senor, we are much in your debt.'

'Saw what was going on and thought it didn't look just right,' Hatfield answered. 'Thought I'd better take a hand. How many men did you lose?'

'Three are dead,' the Mexican replied, his face grim. 'Two more are wounded, not seriously, I believe, *El Dios* be praised.'

'Bring them over here and I'll try to patch them up,' Hatfield ordered. He whistled for Goldy who trotted to him, whinnying softly.

From his saddle pouches Hatfield took a roll of bandage and a pot of antiseptic ointment, with which he treated and bound up the flesh wounds of the two drivers.

'That should hold them till they see a doctor,' he told the Mexican. 'Now let's have a look at those two hellions I downed. By the way, whose train is this?'

'It is owned by my *patron*, Sebastian Gomez,' the other replied. 'I'm Miguel Allende, the captain of the guards.'

'Guards? Where do they ride, on the carts?' Hatfield asked.

'*Si*, Senor, with the drivers.'

'A perfect setup for the raiders,' Hatfield commented. 'You never had a chance.'

'That is true,' Miguel Allende admitted ruefully.

Hatfield led the way to where the two dead drygulchers lay. One was a lanky, nondescript looking individual whom Hatfield immediately dismissed as ordinary border scum. The other, slighter in build, interested him. He had graying hair, neatly trimmed, a sharply pointed nose and a short, grizzled beard that somehow struck Hatfield as being out of place on his sallow face. He moved the body a little so that the light from the burning cart fell full upon it.

'Look around and see if you can find a pair of glasses,' he told Miguel.

'I see none,' the other said, after searching the ground carefully.

'Well, this jigger wore a pair, and recently,' Hatfield said.

'Senor, how do you know?' Miguel asked wonderingly.

Hatfield pointed to the flesh in back of the dead man's temples.

'See the little ridges there?' he explained. 'He wore steel framed glasses most of the time and the frames were rather tight. The thin steel rods of the frames indented the flesh slightly and caused those little ridges to form in the course of time. See, there are tiny furrows marked plainly in the flesh.'

Miguel bent closer. 'It is true,' he admitted.

11

'Now that you point it out it is quite plain to see. I would never have noticed it. You have remarkable eyes, Senor.'

'They'll do,' Hatfield said. 'Wonder what these guys have in their pockets.'

An assortment of odds and ends were revealed, including a surprisingly large sum of money in gold and silver.

'These hellions never got all that following the tail of a cow,' Hatfield muttered. 'Hello, what's this?'

He'd drawn a neat leather case from the small man's buttoned down shirt pocket. It contained a deck of playing cards. They were good cards, a brand Hatfield did not recall seeing before. He ran his sensitive fingertips over the backs of several before he recased them, his brows knitting a little. He proceeded to give special attention to the dead man's hands. They were soft, well cared for, with long supple fingers, the nails cut very short. He spoke to Miguel, who knelt beside him.

'Ever see this one before?' he asked.

Miguel rubbed the bridge of his nose and looked thoughtful. 'Somehow I feel vaguely that I have,' he replied in his precise mission school English. 'Or someone he resembled. The feeling one has when passing by a spot one is sure has never before been visited, but that appears familiar, and at the same time different.'

Hatfield nodded, his own eyes thoughtful.

'Jigger would look a mite different wearing glasses and without whiskers,' he observed.

'You think he did not always wear the beard?'

'He hasn't been wearing this one long,' Hatfield replied definitely. He parted the short, scraggly whiskers. 'You'll notice the skin under the hair is almost as dark as over his cheekbones,' he pointed out. 'If he'd worn a beard for long, the skin of his cheeks and chin would be several degrees lighter. This is a growth of only a few weeks, I'd say.'

'It is even so,' conceded Miguel. 'I try to see him as he might have been and I seem to look upon that one.'

Hatfield unravelled the complicated phraseology and decided Miguel meant he did recall somebody who looked like the dead owlhoot.

'Call the boys over for a look,' he suggested.

But the other carters could see nothing familiar about either of the dead men. Hatfield began replacing the contents of their pockets, except the cased deck of cards, which he slipped into his own pocket.

'Souvenir,' he explained. Miguel nodded understanding.

'I once knew an hombre who cut off the ears of those he slayed,' he remarked. 'He dried them and kept them in his pocket. Sometimes, when the mescal had warmed his blood, he would take one out and chew it.'

13

Hatfield chuckled. 'We'll leave this pair, ears and all, for the sheriff to look over,' he decided.

The carters jumped nervously as a raucous bray sounded from the brush nearby.

'Must be that darn mule I took the header over,' Hatfield said. 'Round him up, and while you're at it, see if you can find the horses this pair rode. Brands might tell us something.'

The mule was easily caught, but no trace was found of the two horses.

'Well-trained critters and they followed the others when they hightailed, the chances are,' Hatfield decided. He gazed at the dead men for a moment.

'Funny one, this,' he mused apropos of the smaller man, 'a gambler—dealer, I'd say— packing his own private marked deck and riding with a bunch of hard-shooting drygulchers. Some sort of a peculiar tie-up, judging from what shows on the surface. Might prove important. Sort of masterminding the bunch, perhaps, or representing somebody who does.'

He turned to the huddled carters. 'Let's see if we can get those overturned buggies back on their wheels,' he suggested.

After considerable labor they got the carts righted, the bales of goods back in place.

'How come that one caught fire?' Hatfield asked, pointing to the smoldering wreckage.

'The *ladrones* threw a lighted torch into it

14

right after they started shooting,' Miguel replied. 'It was loaded with wool and tallow.'

'The only one packing that kind of a load?'

'*Si*, the only one,' Miguel said. Hatfield nodded.

'Looks like they either made a lucky hit or knew just which one to fire,' he commented. 'Suppose this train is headed for Sanders?'

'That is so,' Miguel replied, casting a worried glance along the trail. He voiced the general apprehension.

'Senor, do you think those *ladrones* will come back?'

'Not likely,' Hatfield decided. 'I figure they got a belly full.'

He studied the carters a moment. They were nervous, jumpy and generally demoralized.

'Miguel,' he said, 'I don't think it's a good idea for you to head to Sanders tonight. I've a notion you fellows aren't in much shape to make the drive. Besides, those three dead men should be taken to town. Suppose you turn around and head back to Aguilar?'

'Senor, I believe the thought is good,' Miguel instantly agreed. 'I am sure *Don* Sebastian will understand.'

'Reckon he will, especially after I've had a talk with him,' Hatfield said. 'Okay, let's get going. Isn't very far, is it?'

'But a few miles,' Miguel answered. He shouted orders to the drivers, who looked decidedly relieved as they turned their clumsy vehicles and got the mules headed south.

Were Miguel Allende not so perturbed over what had happened, he might have paused to wonder just why he was taking orders from this tall, level-eye cowhand who apparently had usurped all the authority in sight. Other and more important folk had wondered the same thing but they, too, did just what Jim Hatfield told them to do.

With much creaking and groaning of wheels and tires, heartfelt curses by the drivers and cheerful snorting on the part of the mules, who visioned comfortable stalls and fodder much sooner than they had expected, the train got under way. Hatfield rode a little distance behind the rearmost cart, where he could keep an eye on everything that went on. He didn't expect the drygulchers to play a return engagement, with or without reinforcements, but such gentry were sometimes known to do the unexpected; he was taking no chances.

'Well,' he remarked to Goldy, 'Captain Bill wasn't fooling when he said this was a lively section down here. Barely hit it and I'm in the middle of a raid. Appears to be a plumb interesting country.'

A bit too interesting, some folks might have thought, but the man the Texas Rangers had named the Lone Wolf appeared pleased at the prospect.

16

CHAPTER TWO

As he lounged comfortably in his high-pommeled saddle, Hatfield reviewed the salient points of his interview with Captain McDowell when the famed Commander of the Border Battalion handed him his latest assignment.

'Jim, what do you know about the Chihuahua Trail country between Presidio and Sanders?' Captain Bill asked.

'Not a great deal,' Hatfield replied. 'I've been at Presidio a couple of times, and I visited Sanders once. To the north of Sanders, you know, the C & P Railroad tentatively plans the route for its new line to the west.'

'Don't reckon you're overly well known in that section, then,' remarked Captain Bill.

'Reckon that's right,' Hatfield conceded. 'Of course it's the sort of country where there are lots of comings and goings, but I can say I'm not acquainted with the residents down there and I suppose they don't know me.'

'Sounds pretty good,' nodded Captain Bill. 'I've been getting a lot of letters from down there lately. Seems the infernal cart wars are busting loose again, and strong. Folks kicking about robberies and shootings and holdups. Some been hurt who haven't anything to do with the rows, and that isn't good. One letter in particular from a feller named Sebastian Gomez. He's complaining to beat the devil. Says his carts have been robbed and wrecked and burned and that the local authorities can't seem to do anything about it. He's yelling for a troop of Rangers pronto to restore order.'

'Price cutting again?' Hatfield asked. 'That's what started the trouble over to Goliad, where twenty men were killed.'

Captain Bill shook his head. 'Doesn't seem to be this time,' he answered. 'From what I understand, Gomez just about has a monopoly of trade from Mexico that comes north by way of Ojinaga on the other side of the Rio Grande, opposite Presidio. The shipments then go north to Sanders and then east to Helena, San Antonio and Goliad.'

'Carting is big business in that section,' Hatfield observed. 'Is Gomez a Mexican?'

'Nope, he was born in Texas, and so was his father before him,' Captain Bill replied. 'Spanish stock, of course, but he's a Texan and has a right to call on us for help.'

Hatfield waited patiently while Captain Bill stuffed black tobacco into a blacker pipe; he knew there was more coming.

'There's another angle to the business, the real reason why I figure to send you down there,' McDowell said when his pipe was drawing to his satisfaction. 'There are folks who have a notion that Gomez is Javelina.'

'The devil you say! The bandit leader?'

'That's right,' said Captain Bill. 'The hellion who's been operating on both sides of the border in the Presidio country, the one we've never been able to get a line on. Wonder why the devil they call him Javelina? That means pig, doesn't it?'

'Not exactly,' Hatfield replied. 'Javelina is a corruption of the Spanish word, *jabelina*, meaning wild sow. To the Mexicans Javelina means pecarry, the little wild pig that travels in bands. Javelinas are vicious and deadly fighters, merciless killers who fear nothing. With their razor-sharp tusks they rip to pieces anything that gets in their way. The wolf and the bear and even the mountain lion hightail when javelinas come along: they know they wouldn't have a chance with the ferocious little devils. So there isn't anything incongruous in the Mexicans calling a snake-blooded, merciless outlaw Javelina.

'Incidentally,' he added, 'I don't believe Javelina is a Mexican, although lots of folks figure he is, because of the name, I reckon.'

'Why not?' asked Captain Bill. 'I always figured he must be.'

'Because he doesn't operate like a Mexican,' Hatfield replied. 'He's too efficient, for one thing. You'll remember Javelina never leaves any witnesses. He's a ruthless killer and, like his namesake, always makes a clean sweep. That isn't the Mexican way. A Mexican outlaw may be salty and bad, but he's seldom that sort

19

of a killer. His irresistible Latin impulse to be dramatic makes him want an audience. After he's finished his chore, he likes to ride away with a flourish of his sombrero, with those he's robbed watching him go. He'll kill if he has to, but seldom just to kill. And he never worries much about somebody recognizing him some time. That's *mañana*, and tomorrow never comes. I'd bet a hat full of pesos that Javelina is from north of the Rio Grande.'

'Could be,' admitted Captain Bill. 'Anyhow, he's a darned nuisance and we've got to drop a loop on him. Of course, the talk about Gomez being Javelina may be just talk, but we can't afford to overlook any leads. And that's what I'm coming to.

'As I said, I got a letter from Gomez. May seem funny, if he should happen to be Javelina, that he'd write asking for Rangers, but it could be a bluff, aimed to distract suspicion from himself. Especially as he very likely knows I haven't any troop of Rangers to send right now. What he doesn't know is that I've got one Ranger I can spare. So I did a bit of thinking. I know a feller at Sanders who deals with Gomez, feller by the name of Tom Conley. We used to ride together for the old Bar W, before I got in the Rangers. I got in touch with Conley and put a flea in his ear. Conley had been complaining to Gomez about his shipments being delayed because of the trouble. He suggested to Gomez that he hire a

20

good straight-shooting gunfighter to take charge of his carts, to act as a foreman. Gomez agreed it was a good notion and asked Conley if he knew a man. Conley told him he did and figured he could get him. So you're going to see Gomez with a letter from Conley recommending you for the chore. If folks down there don't know you're a Ranger, maybe you can keep under cover for a spell and learn something. Okay?'

'Be ready to ride in the morning,' Hatfield replied.

'Fine!' said Captain Bill, adding cheerfully, 'It's a nice country with nice people— smugglers, wideloopers, gunslingers, owlhoots, and so on. Down there's where they fight the Helena Duel. If a couple of gents fall out over something, they tie their left hands together, give 'em each a knife with a three inch blade, whirl 'em around a few times and turn 'em loose. With the short blade there ain't much chance of a fatal stroke first off so they go on slashing and hacking till loss of blood finishes one or both. Never any quarter given or expected, and usually both cash in. If one happens to survive, you can tell ever afterward he was in one of those fights. Looks like he ate his way through a plate glass window. Real nice people! Yes, you ought to have a fine time down there. Of course, if things get too much for you to handle, let out a yelp and I'll take a day off and come down myself and straighten 'em out.'

'I'll do that,' Hatfield promised seriously.

Captain Bill chuckled and waved him from the office.

Hatfield came back to the present as the string of carts came to a long rise. He quickened Goldy's pace and when the foremost cart reached the crest he was riding beside it. On the far slope the moonlit trail stretched deserted, with nothing near it to provide cover. In the distance was a cluster of lights that Hatfield knew must be the town of Aguilar, where Captain McDowell said Sebastian Gomez had his headquarters.

An hour later the carts rumbled along the dusty main street of the cow town. People on the sidewalks shouted questions that the carters answered with profane explanations of what had happened.

'Take the carts to the station and stable the mules,' Miguel told them. 'And now, Senor, if you are willing, we will visit the sheriff.'

They found the sheriff in his office in front of the jail, getting ready to close up for the day. He was a grizzled old frontiersman with a bad-tempered face and a truculent eye. Hatfield decided that he was of a suspicious nature and saw little good in anybody. His first remark, after Miguel had finished telling him of the raid, confirmed the Ranger's estimation.

'So you barged right into the shindig, eh?' he said. 'You fellers who are always taking the

22

law in your own hands sooner or later end in trouble. Law enforcement is for properly accredited peace officers.'

'That's what I told them, but they wouldn't wait till I came and got you and kept right on shooting at the carters,' Hatfield replied without a smile.

The sheriff flushed. 'Don't go getting funny,' he growled. 'I ain't saying you didn't do a good job this time, but the next time you might find yourself taking up for the wrong bunch. Ever think of that?'

'I have,' Hatfield admitted, 'but so far I've been lucky.'

'Maybe your luck won't hold,' said the sheriff. 'Okay, I'll ride down there in the morning and pick up the bodies. I'll want you fellers here for the inquest.' He glanced toward the cell doors as he spoke.

'You won't need to lock me up, I'll be here,' Hatfield smiled.

'Who the hell said anything about locking you up?' snorted the sheriff. 'You don't look like a liar, anyway. Miguel, you'd better send somebody out to Gomez' ranch to notify him of what happened. I suppose he'll come in raring and charging and accusing me of not keeping order.'

Despite his truculence, the sheriff did not appear to be looking forward to the coming interview with unqualified delight. Hatfield suddenly felt sorry for him.

'Honest and salty, but sort of behind the door when they were handing out brains,' he mused, adding, 'and I've a notion there are plenty of brains operating in this section right now.'

As they left the office, Hatfield turned to Miguel. 'I want to stable my horse and then find a place where I can put on the feedbag, too,' he said.

'There is plenty of room for the *caballo* in the big barn where we keep the mules, and he will receive the care due such a beautiful animal—I never saw a finer,' replied Miguel. 'Then we will go to the Last Chance saloon that is run by the Senor Steve Ennis. Both food and drink are of the best.'

The freight station proved to be a long, rambling building with a corral in back. Nearby was a barn in which Goldy found suitable accommodations. Hatfield made sure that all his needs were taken care of and then joined Miguel who had paused to dispatch a rider to notify Gomez of the raid.

'The *patron* owns a ranch to the northeast of here,' he explained. 'It is a good holding. His *casa* is nearly fifteen miles distant, so I doubt that he will come to town before morning. Now let us eat.'

Through narrow, twisting streets, poorly lighted by an occasional lantern hung on a pole, they made their way. On either side were dark warehouse buildings, rude shacks, adobes and walled corrals. Hatfield realized that Aguilar was a much larger town than he had expected.

'It is the supply center for a wide and prosperous cattle and mining region,' Miguel replied to his comment. 'Also the freighting business from all directions center here. And, not altogether to the advantage of peace and harmony, the Chihuahua and other trails pass this way. We get some unusual hombres here from time to time, from Mexico, the west and the north. You noticed a few earlier in the evening.'

'If that bunch was a fair sample, I've a notion you don't hit it far wrong in your estimate,' Hatfield replied. 'By the way, Miguel, where did you learn to speak English? You're from Mexico, aren't you?'

'*Si*, I am from the land of *mañana*, as you call it,' Miguel replied. 'I was brought up by the good Fathers of the Mission of *San Francisco de los Julimes* who were skilled in languages. There is a disadvantage, though,' he added with a slightly wry smile. 'At times my own countrymen are puzzled by my Spanish and many Americans look blank at my English. It is indeed a pleasure to meet one who understands both.'

Hatfield laughed. 'And Gomez is also an educated man, I presume?'

'Yes,' replied Miguel, 'and travelled and very wise. I trust you will like the *patron*, as we call him. Well, here is the Last Chance. Why it is so named I do not know; there are plenty more drinking places farther down the street.'

He had stopped before a rambling building with plate glass windows and an elaborate false-front. The room they entered was brightly lighted, larger and more lavishly furnished than most of the cow town saloons with which Hatfield had had experience, but the patrons were typical of cattle country. Many turned to stare at them as they pushed through the swinging doors; evidently the story of the raid had gotten around.

They had just seated themselves at a table when a man came striding across the room to greet them. He was not a big man but his slender, well-knit broad-shouldered figure gave an impression of steely power held in leash. He was dressed in black from broad-brimmed slouch hat to highly polished boots, the funereal hue of his costume relieved only by the snow of his ruffled shirt front. His eyes were pale blue, very keen and very critical. His skin was the clear bronze that only blonde coloring exposed to much wind and sun can achieve, his hair yellow and inclined to curl. He had a straight nose and a firm, thin-lipped mouth. He looked a gentleman, and, Hatfield decided, perhaps was one.

'Hello, Miguel,' he said in a pleasantly modulated voice, 'hear you had a bit of trouble.'

'Even so, Senor,' Miguel replied. 'If it were not for my amigo here, it would doubtless have been much worse.' He turned to Hatfield. 'This is the Senor Ennis of whom I spoke.'

Hatfield introduced himself and they shook hands. Ennis had a firm and powerful grip, but not to a degree that hinted at affectation.

'You did a splendid job, Mr. Hatfield, and rid the community of a couple of pests. A pity you didn't down a few more. The affair was deplorable. Business rivalry is all right, but not to the extent where it condones the extremes of violence.'

Miguel apparently read significance in the words, for his lips compressed and he remarked, 'The *patron* did not seek conditions that exist, nor does he approve of them.'

'I doubt if anybody approves of them, but they do exist,' said Ennis. 'Things have been allowed to get out of hand and something must be done. Hope you'll see fit to coil your twine with us for a spell, Mr. Hatfield. We need men like you. I'll send over a drink.'

With a friendly nod he returned to the far end of the bar, where he engaged in conversation with various patrons.

'He is a nice man,' said Miguel, 'but I fear he has a poor opinion of all freighters. Which, however, is not surprising when one considers the happenings of recent months,' he added with a sigh.

While they discussed their food, Hatfield

27

took note of the saloon and its occupants. There was a long mirror-blazing bar, a lunch counter, a dance floor, numerous gaming tables, a couple of roulette wheels, a faro bank, as well as tables for eating. All in all, a busy and prosperous establishment he decided, and typically cow country.

The patrons interested him more. The majority were undoubtedly cowhands, rollicking young fellows out for an evening's diversion. There was also a group he decided were teamsters and other employees of the freighting outfits. A few woolen-shirted and corduroyed individuals he catalogued as miners. A number of Mexicans in velvet pantaloons, steeple sombreros, jackets gay with embroidery and hempen sandals caught his eye. They were not *vaqueros*—Mexican cowboys—he felt sure. Doubtless they too were connected with the freighting business.

There were also quite a few individuals who dressed like cowhands but who, the Ranger decided, were not or hadn't been for a long time. These interested him most of all. 'Sunset to sunrise riders.'

Suddenly the swinging doors banged open and a big beefy man entered and looked around as one who invites contradiction. He had a square, blocky face, intolerant black eyes and a tight-lipped mouth. As his eyes rested on the table Hatfield and Miguel occupied, his scowl deepened. However, he did not pause but continued to the bar and ordered whiskey in a rumbling voice.

'Who is the bad-tempered gent?' Hatfield asked. 'Appears he doesn't like one or both of us.'

'He doesn't like me and you being in my company is sufficient to cause him not to like you,' Miguel replied. 'That's Kane Fisher. He owns a freighting business. His wagons carry supplies to the mines west of here and to outlying ranches. He also freights goods to San Antonio and Goliad and to and from the quicksilver mines at Terlingua. He tried to take some of the *patron*'s Presidio business and there were words.'

'I suppose there was no harm in trying, just so long as he did it in an ethical manner,' Hatfield commented. 'Did he offer to cut prices?'

'He did,' answered Miguel. 'However, the traders south of the Border are loyal to the *patron* and refused his offer, for the time being, at least.'

Miguel did not elaborate on the last statement and Hatfield refrained from questioning him although his eyes grew thoughtful. Here was an angle Captain McDowell evidently didn't know about. And the making of trouble or he was much mistaken. Fisher had the appearance of one who would not easily concede defeat.

Hatfield noted that Steve Ennis was

regarding Fisher with unfriendly eyes. Miguel noted the direction of his glance.

'Bad blood between those two,' he remarked. 'When Fisher drinks or gambles he gets ugly and has more than once started trouble here. Doubtless Ennis would prefer he didn't come in at all, but Fisher is influential and a bad hombre to have for an enemy.'

'See he isn't staying long,' Hatfield observed as Fisher, after gulping a couple of drinks, stalked out. He did not glance at their table.

Miguel pushed back his plate with a satisfied sigh and ordered drinks.

'If it is agreeable with you, we will wait another hour and if the *patron* does not appear and we hear no word from him, we will go to bed,' he said.

'Suits me,' Hatfield agreed. 'I didn't get much shut-eye last night and I was in the saddle since daybreak. I'll have to look up a place to pound my ear.'

'There is a rooming house near the freight station where you can secure comfortable accommodations,' Miguel suggested.

'That'll be fine,' Hatfield replied.

They passed the time sipping wine and discussing the freighting business, Miguel doing most of the talking. Finally he glanced at the clock over the bar.

'It is past the midnight hour,' he observed. 'I am sure the *patron* will not put in an appearance tonight.' He beckoned a waiter to

30

bring their bill. 'No! No!' he said. 'You can pay for nothing. Tonight you are my guest. I insist that it be so.'

'Okay, if you feel that way about it,' Hatfield smiled. *'Gracias!'*

'It is to you the thanks are due,' Miguel said with an answering smile.

They left the saloon and walked along the gloomy streets toward the station.

'Senor,' Miguel suddenly said in a low voice, 'there are three men standing in the shadow of that building, just this side of the light. They appear to be waiting for someone.'

'So I noticed,' Hatfield replied. 'And as it happens, there are three more sliding along behind us a little ways; I've been watching their shadows on the buildings across the street. May not mean anything, but then again, it may. Quick, into this alley, and keep going!'

They whirled into the alley they were just passing and ran down it at top speed. From behind them there was a shout.

The alley was short and opened onto a street that paralleled the one they just left. Miguel was heading for it when Hatfield jerked him back.

'That's what they'll expect us to do,' he whispered. 'Here, into this crack between the buildings, and keep still.'

They squeezed into the narrow opening and stood motionless. Hatfield loosened his guns in their sheaths.

31

For a few minutes there was silence, then they heard stealthy steps coming up the alley. There was a sharp exclamation, followed by a blast of gunfire that was instantly answered by shots from the other end of the alley. For a moment the shooting continued, then a voice yelled something and it ceased as suddenly as it had begun. A mutter of voices reached the ears of the tense listeners crouched between the buildings. A moment later fast steps faded up the alley.

'Just as I figured,' Hatfield chuckled softly. 'The two bunches barged into one another and each thought the other was us. Hope somebody shot straight. Let's go outside, and head back to the main street where it's light. We'll make it to your rooming house by some other route, although I expect those drygulching gents kept on going.'

Walking fast they turned a corner and heard shouting from the direction of the main street. Evidently the shooting had attracted attention. Rounding another corner, they barged squarely into the sheriff, who was hurrying in the other direction.

'So!' he exclaimed, 'Been starting something else, eh? Where did you leave the bodies?'

'Why, Sheriff, I'm surprised at you thinking we'd do such things,' Hatfield protested mildy. 'We just heard some shooting over on the next street and came away in a hurry lest we might get mixed up in it and you'd accuse us of taking the law in our own hands again.'

The sheriff swore and looked suspicious. 'Oh, tarnation! Why don't you go to bed so I can get some sleep?' he demanded.

'We're going to do that, right away,' Miguel promised. '*Buenas noches*, Sheriff Thomas.'

'It's a bad night if you're asking me,' snorted the sheriff as he turned the corner.

'It seems news gets around fast in this section,' Hatfield remarked as they neared the rooming house beside the freight station. 'And it would also seem that those gents who made the drygulching try down on the trail circled back to town. Appears they or some of their friends were out to even up the score.'

'It is even so,' Miguel agreed, his eyes worried. 'I fear that by lending us a helping hand you have brought grave danger upon yourself. Perhaps it would be better if you rode away quickly and at once.'

'Too tired,' Hatfield replied cheerfully. 'Besides, I promised the sheriff I'd be in town for the inquest tomorrow. Right now if I don't find a bed in a hurry I'm going to be asleep standing up.'

The bed, a comfortable one, was quickly forthcoming and Hatfield proceeded to put it to good use. He was asleep almost before his head hit the pillow.

CHAPTER THREE

Meanwhile there was an angry discussion going on in the back room of a dingy, little *pulqueria* on the outskirts of the town. Kane Fisher, scowling and muttering, strode up and down with nervous, jerky steps. From time to time he would frown balefully at half a dozen men who sat at a table littered with bottles and glasses. One, mumbling under his breath, kept swabbing at a bullet-gashed cheek. Another had a bandaged arm in a rude sling.

'You must be proud of yourselves!' Fisher suddenly barked. 'Six of you against the two of them and you bungle it. End up gunning each other while they stood back somewhere and laughed. Of all the terrapin-brained sons of jackasses you're the limit!'

'I wish you'd been there with lead whistling all around you. Maybe you wouldn't talk so big,' the man with the wounded cheek replied.

'If I'd been there the job wouldn't have been bungled,' Fisher declared angrily. 'And what happened down there on the trail? I suppose you never thought to keep an eye on your back track to make sure somebody wasn't trailing you or there wasn't an outrider pacing the train.'

'Like hell we didn't!' the wounded man growled. 'There was nobody behind us and there was nobody out on the prairie when we holed up. That big hellion just dropped from nowhere.'

'I still can't understand why you didn't stand and shoot it out with him,' bawled Fisher, pausing to hammer the table with his big fist. 'There was six of you handling that chore, too, or trying to handle it.'

'Shoot it out with him,' snorted the other, 'he was back in the brush and that infernal sulphur-colored horse was doing a dance like a jack rabbit on a hot skillet, and the blasted carters were getting the range. We were caught in a crossfire and if we hadn't hightailed there wouldn't be any of us here to tell you about it.'

'Which might not be so bad,' said Fisher in what was about as near a snarl as the human voice is capable of. 'Well, anyhow, you bungled both jobs and that big hellion is still running around loose. If you'd done him in tonight Gomez might have trouble getting another gunslinger to do his fighting for him.'

'You really think Gomez brought him in?' asked a small wizened man with cold, dead-looking eyes.

'Of course he did—who else?' replied Fisher. 'He didn't drop from the sky, and if he was just a wandering cowhand, would he have mixed into that rukus? He would not! He'd have hightailed away from there like anybody who isn't plumb loco. Of course Gomez brought him in, and he's salty, and from the looks of him he's got brains, something this outfit needs blamed bad.'

'Uh-huh, I agree with you there,' nodded the wizened man. 'I think it was a mistake at the start, taking Gomez on.'

'Taking Gomez on, heck!' bawled Fisher, hammering the table again. 'Who wrecked our wagons and shot two of our drivers? Who held up a train and carted off a valuable shipment? Who tipped off the Customs agents and caused us to near get caught with a load of contraband? Gomez! Couldn't have been anybody else. He started things, and I aim to finish them. I don't give a hang if he is Javelina, as folks say. When I've finished with him he'll be out of the freighting business, and don't you forget it.'

'Kane, it might be a good notion to pipe down a mite,' remarked the wounded man with a nervous glance at the closed door. 'They can hear you clear up to the Last Chance.'

'Besides,' said the wizened man, who appeared argumentative, 'there's no proof Gomez is responsible for what happened to our trains. It could have been somebody else.'

'Who, I'd like to know?' demanded Fisher, adding with a sneer, 'What the devil's the matter with you, Malone, your nerve giving out?'

'No, it ain't,' retorted Malone, 'and my brain ain't giving out, either. I still think tangling with Gomez is a mistake. We were

36

doing all right as it was, and you had to go and try and horn in on his range and get him riled. You know, Kane, a big hog sometimes gets his feet in the trough and turns it over, and then everybody goes hungry. Oh, don't worry! I'm with you to the finish, no matter how loco you go. Doesn't make any difference to me what happens, not any more. I stopped living quite a spell back, Kane, when I first stepped outside the straight trail. I'm just a corpse walking around. But there's one little thing you might remember, Kane, when you get to talking big. A corpse sometimes sort of hankers for company!'

Fisher flushed darkly, but something in Malone's dead eyes made him pause. He rubbed the back of his neck vigorously, as if it suddenly felt cold.

'No sense in fighting among ourselves,' he said in an altered tone. 'We've got to pull together. Okay, Malone, you've got the most savvy of this bunch. I want you to keep tabs on that big hellion. Let me know everything you learn and what moves he figures to make, if you can find out. I'll see what I can make of him myself next time.'

'Okay,' nodded Malone, 'but I've a notion you're taking on a hefty chore. Think it's safe to ride to the trail, now? We've got a little job there to attend to. No sense in leaving possible evidence against us layin' round.'

'Let's go,' grunted Fisher. 'Getting along

toward morning and we want to be in the clear before it's light.'

They filed out of the saloon. A few minutes later fast hoof beats faded away into the northeast.

CHAPTER FOUR

Sunlight like a flood of molten gold was streaming through the window when Hatfield awoke. For several minutes he lay comfortably drowsy, idly watching the patterns the sunbeams made on the garishly flowered carpet and pondering the fact that intense light can make anything beautiful, even such a monstrosity of clashing colors as that carpet. Rousing a bit, he reviewed the happenings of the previous night. He chuckled, remembering the cantankerous sheriff and his caustic remarks about folks who took the law in their own hands.

Just the same, however, that remark stirred a chord of memory. It was as an echo to Captain Bill McDowell's warning, quite a few years before, when young Jim Hatfield, just graduated from engineering college and seething with wrath over the wanton murder of his father by wideloopers, was called to Ranger headquarters.

'Aim to ride the vengeance trail, eh, Jim?'

Captain Bill had said. 'A bad trail to ride, Jim. Taking the law in your own hands is risky business and sometimes finds you on the wrong side of the law. A bad business.'

'Those snake-blooded bushwackers aren't going to get away with it, sir,' Hatfield heard himself reply.

'I don't want them to,' said Captain Bill. 'Your dad was my friend, but I don't want my old friend's son heading the wrong way. Oh, I know you're going after them, and nothing I can say will stop you, but I got a suggestion to make. There's a right way to do the chore. Come into the Rangers, Jim, and go after your dad's killers with all the power and prestige of the State of Texas behind you. I'll hand you the job soon as your commission is signed. After you've finished it, if you don't like the service and hanker to go ahead and be an engineer, okay, you can quit and no hard feelings.'

Hatfield had taken Captain Bill's advice. As a Texas Ranger he ran down his father's killers and brought them to justice; but it was a long, hard job, and before it was finished, Hatfield realized that he didn't want to leave the Rangers, not just yet. He was young and there was plenty of time later to follow the profession for which he had been educated. He'd just stick with the Rangers for a while.

This, he realized was what Captain McDowell had planned from the first. He had never regretted his decision, and now the Lone Wolf was admired and respected by honest men everywhere, and equally feared and hated by the outlaw breed. His exploits were legend throughout Texas and he was in line for McDowell's post when the old commander decided to resign. He still planned to be an engineer some day and had kept up his studies, finding his knowledge useful quite a few times in the course of his Ranger activities.

Hatfield had just finished washing up and dressing when a knock on the door sounded. He opened it to admit Miguel, his face shining from a vigorous application of soap and water.

'The *patron* has arrived,' he announced. 'He is having breakfast at the Last Chance and sends word that he will be honored if you will join him.'

'Be right with you,' Hatfield replied. 'I can stand a helping myself about now. Let's go.'

Sebastian Gomez looked the *hidalgo* with his flashing black eyes, his lean figure, black hair liberally sprinkled with gray and dark, finely chiselled features. He wore the prosperous ranch owner's garb with the same careless grace with which his Spanish forebears wore shining armor. There was a bitter twist to his lips, however, the significance of which Hatfield understood.

Old time Border dwellers, in whose hearts the grim memories of Gonad and The Alamo lingered long, firmly believed the only good

40

Mexican was a dead Mexican. Many of them passed the sentiment along to the next generation. Now the unjust feeling was dying out, but it had not yet been entirely eradicated. To most Texans, Sebastian Gomez, though Texas born, was, because of his Spanish blood, a Mexican. Undoubtedly he had met with more than one unpleasant experience, which was liable to leave a mark on a proud and sensitive nature. And Hatfield knew that the resulting brooding sometimes took strange turns and the innocent might well suffer along with the guilty. While he regarded Gomez with an open mind, he did not fail to take latent possibilities into consideration.

Miguel performed the introductions and then departed. Gomez' acknowledgment was courteously reserved but not lacking in warmth.

'Pull up a chair, Mr. Hatfield,' he invited. 'First off I want to thank you for what you did last night. It was a splendid act, going to the aid of strangers and exposing yourself to great personal danger.'

'Yes, they were strangers, but in a way they weren't,' Hatfield smiled reply. 'I had a pretty good notion that they must have been one of your trains and—I have a letter for you, sir.'

Gomez looked astonished, but as he read the letter Hatfield handed him, his eyes brightened.

'So you are the man Tom Conley spoke of!'

he exclaimed. 'Well, I've always highly esteemed Conley's judgment, and my regard certainly isn't lessened. You'll take the job?' he added eagerly, 'after what happened last night?'

'Yes, I'll take it,' Hatfield replied, 'on the condition that I'm allowed to handle the chore as I see fit.'

'You certainly will be,' Gomez declared with emphasis, 'but let's have some breakfast; then we can talk.'

Gomez proved a charming host, tacitly avoiding business matters until the meal was finished.

'And now?' he said, smiling his slightly wry smile.

'First off, sir, I'd like to ask a few questions. To begin with, have you any idea who was responsible for the attack on your train last night?'

Gomez hesitated, pinching his chin with his thumb and forefinger.

'I think,' Hatfield said quietly, 'that if I am to handle your trains I am entitled to know just what I'm up against.'

'I suppose so,' admitted Gomez, evidently still reluctant to speak out. He drew a deep breath and said, 'I am not given to making accusations that I am unable to prove, but I will say that not until after I had a business difference with Kane Fisher did I begin having trouble.'

'What kind of a difference?' Hatfield asked.

'Fisher approached some of my accounts and offered to transport their northbound goods for less money,' Gomez replied.

'I see,' Hatfield nodded. 'And they turned him down?'

'Yes,' said Gomez. 'I have served them for many years and they had no desire to make a change, even at a lower cost. When I heard about it, I reproached Fisher for what I considered an underhanded procedure.'

Hatfield nodded again. 'But perhaps Fisher didn't look at it in that light,' he commented. 'He may have considered it only a legitimate exercise of competition.'

'It would appear he did,' Gomez replied. 'I give him credit for sincerity there. He angrily contended that he had a right to try and pick up business anywhere he could and pointed out that I had no contracts with the shippers and therefore it was an open market. He also said that with his large wagons and more efficient packing and operation he could afford to transport the goods cheaper. I fear there was something of truth in his contention.'

Hatfield nodded. The new against the old. Even without active enmity on the part of Fisher, or somebody, he could foresee trouble for Gomez.

'Doubtless your father was in the carting business before you,' he observed.

'That is right,' Gomez agreed. 'Some of my shippers south of the Border dealt with him.'

'How about the dealers at this end of the line?' Hatfield asked.

'There's where I'm afraid I may have trouble,' Gomez explained ruefully. 'They are getting impatient over delays, with me and with Fisher, also.'

Hatfield looked up, and asked an oblique question, 'Your trains the only ones that have had trouble?'

Again Gomez seemed to hesitate. 'No, they are not,' he said slowly. 'Fisher has also had trouble. In fact, he had it first. Three of his wagons were wrecked and two of his drivers shot. Another train was robbed.'

'Before or after you had the row with him?' Hatfield asked quietly.

Gomez flushed a little. 'It was after we had the talk,' he admitted.

'Then you had trouble?'

'That is right.'

Hatfield tried a shot in the dark. 'And then Fisher had more trouble?'

Again Gomez was forced to admit it was so. 'But I assure you I did not attack Fisher's train,' he added.

Hatfield nodded without comment. Gomez gave the impression of telling the truth, but Hatfield took into consideration the fact that if he had something to conceal, he could hardly be expected to confide in one who was still a stranger to him. And if he was telling the truth, a disturbing complication had appeared in an already disturbing situation. He rolled and lighted a cigarette. Gomez filled a pipe and they smoked in silence for several minutes. It was broken by Sheriff Thomas who came striding into the saloon in a way that bespoke irritation. He nodded to Gomez, then looked at Hatfield with a disapproving eye.

'About those two jiggers you and Miguel said you did for up on the trail last night,' he said without preamble, 'sure you didn't dream that part of the yarn?'

'Well, if we did, about twenty carters had the same dream,' Hatfield replied. 'Why?'

'Why? Because there ain't no bodies there. I rode up there this morning and found what was left of the burned cart, all right, but nothing else. Guess your three boys will be the only exhibits at the inquest, Gomez. Coroner's jury sets at one o'clock, Hatfield. Be there! I'd figured on having a full house, but I reckon I'll have to make out with three-of-a-kind.'

Without further remark, he turned and strode out.

'Our good sheriff has a rather grisly sense of humor,' Gomez remarked with his wry smile. 'Well, seeing as you and Miguel must be present at the inquest, with perhaps others of the guards and drivers subject to call, there is no use trying to move the train today. I deplore the delay, but I am expecting more carts up from the south before nightfall. We can start them all for Sanders first thing in the morning. I don't think I'll risk another night drive just yet. Would you like to walk over to the station and meet the men there?'

'Yes,' Hatfield answered, 'and I also want to have a talk with the guards. I suppose you have horses at your spread.'

'I have,' Gomez replied. 'Good stock.'

'I'll want as many as there are guards assigned to the train,' Hatfield said. 'There'll be no more squatting on drivers' seats like setting quail from now on.'

Gomez looked a bit startled, but he only remarked, 'You will have complete control of the trains; handle them in whatever manner you see fit.'

'I noticed your hands are all Mexicans,' Hatfield observed as they rose to go.

'Those assigned to the train you contacted are,' Gomez replied. 'There are only Americans with the train coming up from the south today.'

'Why not mix 'em up?' Hatfield asked.

'Why, I've always thought it best to keep the two nationalities separated,' Gomez replied.

Hatfield turned suddenly, and the freighter got the full force of his level green eyes.

'That's foolishness and old-fashioned thinking,' the Lone Wolf said harshly. 'When men work and fight and overcome difficulty and danger side by side, they quickly forget all

46

about such small matters as on which side of a river they happen to have been born. I want mixed crews from now on.'

Gomez looked even more startled than before, and a trifle bewildered, but apparently decided not to argue the point.

'Very well,' he conceded. 'Let's get over to the station.'

As they turned the corner to the street that ran past the station, Gomez suddenly thought of something. 'Discussing other matters, it slipped from my mind, but I wonder what became of the bodies of the two raiders who died by the trail?'

'Well, I think we can be safe in assuming somebody packed them off before the sheriff got there,' Hatfield replied with a rather grim smile. 'It's sure for certain they didn't walk away.'

'But—but, why?'

'I think the obvious answer is that somebody didn't want them on exhibition here in town,' Hatfield said.

'And that means—' Gomez began.

'It doesn't necessarily mean so,' Hatfield interrupted, 'but it does lead one to suspect that a local outfit was mixed up in that deal last night. Or at least some sort of a local tie-up. Not too obvious, however, I'd say. None of your hands recognized either of them.'

Gomez nodded but did not comment further.

47

When they arrived at the station, Gomez called his men together.

'Most of you have already met the Senor Hatfield, under conditions not easy to forget. From now on he is in full charge of the trains and everything pertaining to them. I expect his orders to be obeyed without question.'

For a moment there was silence, then a chorus of *Vivas* arose. Hatfield suppressed a smile as his keen ears caught a nearby mutter—

'*Sangre de Cristo!* Question his orders? Does the *patron* think we have joined the company of the mad!'

Hatfield beckoned Miguel, whose face seemed to have become one great grin. 'Get your guards together,' he ordered. 'I want to talk to them.'

He eyed the silent group for a moment. They were mostly young men with frank, open faces. Hatfield liked their looks.

'You fellows can ride?' he asked. There was a general nodding of heads.

'And shoot? I want the truth. Your lives may depend on telling it straight.'

'They all shoot well with the *escopeta*,' Miguel answered for them. 'If the distance is not too great.'

'When it's not necessary to allow for wind and trajectory,' Hatfield remarked. 'Well, any work they have to do is likely to be at close range, so it doesn't so much matter. How

48

about six-guns?'

Miguel shrugged with Latin expressiveness. 'They know how to pull the trigger.'

'Okay,' Hatfield nodded. 'Rifles for them.' He turned to Gomez.

'How many carts will make up the train tomorrow, sir?' he asked.

Gomez pondered a moment. 'There should be ninety-seven, I'd say,' he replied.

'Then I'll use ten guards,' Hatfield decided. 'That's enough. Too large a force is apt to be unwieldy. Ten good men properly spaced should be able to handle any chore that happens along. You'll send the horses down this evening?'

'They will be here,' Gomez promised. 'I've a notion to ride with you tomorrow,' he added when the group had dispersed.

Hatfield instantly shook his head. 'Don't want you,' he said. 'I've a notion there might possibly be some concentrated gunning for you if it was known you were with the train. No sense in taking needless chances.'

Gomez pinched his chin. 'You could be right,' he admitted. 'Well, I guess it's about time to get over to the sheriff's office for the inquest. Then I have the unpleasant duty of notifying those poor fellows' next of kin.'

The inquest was informal and short. The jury agreed that the three carters met their death at the hands of parties unknown and recommended that the sheriff run down the

49

killers pronto. A typical cow country rider complimented Hatfield on the part he played in the affair but regretted that he didn't shoot straighter and bag the whole bunch.

CHAPTER FIVE

Late in the afternoon the big train from the south rolled in. The teamsters and guards were hard-bitten individuals of all sizes, shapes and ages. Most of them were Border men, but some were from other parts of the state. One grizzled old fellow with twinkly eyes that looked Hatfield up and down was introduced as Si Perkins, the guard captain.

'So you're the feller we been told was coming to take charge of things,' he remarked. 'Well! Well!'

'Just what do you mean by that, Perkins?' Hatfield asked.

'Oh, nothing much, 'cept I been around considerable,' the oldster replied, adding significantly, 'and I sort of got a reputation for keeping a tight latigo on my jaw.'

'I see,' Hatfield said. 'Suppose we go over to the Last Chance and have a drink and a surrounding of chuck.'

'Best thing you've said yet,' said Perkins. 'I can stand both.'

They found a corner table that was rather

isolated and sat down. Hatfield studied his companion a moment and was satisfied with what he saw.

'Perkins,' he said, 'just what is the setup here?'

'Hatfield, I'm blamed if I know, 'cept that there's the making of big trouble,' Perkins answered. 'Kane Fisher is a hard man and he's sure on the prod against Gomez. And Gomez for all his soft voice and nice ways is a cold proposition. I understand he was sort of wild when he was young. Got around considerable and left his mark here and there. Later on he married and settled down. His wife is dead now but he's got a daughter that I reckon sort of holds him in. He's well fixed, or ought to be. Besides, the freighting business, which I reckon has always paid well, he owns a good ranch. There are some funny stories going around about him, but as to that I ain't saying anything, because I don't know anything. But this row between him and Fisher ain't something you can sneeze off. I ain't got no use for Kane Fisher, but I don't discount his ability. He's salty and he's shrewd, and I don't figger his conscience ever bothers him much.'

'Is Gomez a good man to work for?'

'First rate,' Perkins replied with emphasis. 'He sure treats his hands square. He sort of leans to his Mexican help; by that I mean he associates with 'em more than with us fellers, but nobody can say a word against him. We're

51

all for him to the finish. So you see how the situation stands. Gomez has close to a couple of hundred men working for him who like him. Fisher has half that number, all told, and whether they like him or not they'll stand up for him in a rukus. Let a real row bust loose and you'll have another Goliad affair, and twenty men died in that one.'

'We can do without it,' Hatfield said shortly.

'You're darn right,' Perkins agreed. 'I'm a peaceful man. Going to roll the whole train to Sanders tomorrow?'

'Yes,' Hatfield replied, 'and I want you and four of your men—four who can ride and shoot. Miguel Allende is bringing along four of his.'

'Hmmm!' said Perkins. 'Think ten men will be enough? It's a big train.'

'Ten will be plenty, if they're the right sort,' Hatfield answered.

'I'll pick good ones,' Perkins promised.

The carters were drifting in by twos and threes, and soon the long bar was crowded with them, a boisterous, jovial crowd, but a bunch that could quickly erupt into violence if something didn't go just right, Hatfield decided.

'The boys do most of their drinking here,' Perkins observed. 'They like Steve Ennis—he's a nice feller. He don't stand for no foolishness, though. He hits like a mule kicks and he's chain lightning with a gun. I've a notion maybe he started out as a dealer or a river gambler or something like that. Looks the part.'

'Lots of owners got their start that way,' Hatfield agreed.

The lovely blue dusk was sifting down from the hilltops like impalpable dust when Hatfield and Perkins left the saloon for a breath of air. Along the main street several big freight wagons were rumbling, headed north.

'One of Kane Fisher's trains, a short one,' remarked Perkins. 'Five wagons, but each of 'em can pack as much as half a dozen of our dinky carts, and instead of thirty teamsters he needs only five, which makes a big difference in overhead. I asked Gomez once why he didn't change to wagons. He said his father got along all right with carts so they were good enough for him. He's old-fashioned in too many ways for his own good and doesn't seem to realize that times are changing. Take his agreements with the shippers south of the Rio Grande and the dealers at Sanders and other places. He has no contracts. With old timers, a word of mouth agreement was good as a signed contract, that I'll admit. But new folks are raising up and coming in, on both sides of the Border, and they look at things differently. There didn't used to be much competition. Now there's plenty. I'm scairt he'll have to change his ways of doing business or he'll end up out of business. Fisher or somebody else will take it all away from him.'

53

He watched the big wagons rumbling up the street. 'Ain't turning off to Fisher's station,' he said. 'Reckon they're making a night run to Sanders. It's cooler at night and the mules make better time. And Fisher realizes, if Gomez don't, what it means to deliver his stuff when promised. Sanders is a distributing point and the fellers up there make promises to others. When a train of wagons rolls in from a hundred miles off, they expect to make their pickups and get going on schedule. As I said, I ain't got no use for Fisher, but I respect his business savvy. He's a go-getter and he don't give up easy. He missed his throw when he made a try to drop a loop on some of Gomez' accounts in Mexico, but next time those folks, with delays and non-deliveries making trouble for them, may be more in a mood to listen to his proposition. Oh, well, reckon there's no use bothering my head about it. I'm just guard captain, but maybe you can put a bug in Gomez' ear.'

They walked about for some time, visiting a few places, in some of which the Mexican carters were drinking pulque or playing monte. After a while they returned to the Last Chance.

'Think I could stand a few hands of poker,' said Perkins. 'I'll round up the boys I'm taking along tomorrow and we'll have a game. It'll keep 'em from drinking too much. Care to join us?'

'Not a bad notion,' Hatfield agreed, 'but we'll break it up sort of early; got a hard day ahead of us tomorrow.'

Perkins glanced about as they entered the saloon. 'Don't see Steve Ennis tonight,' he observed. 'He isn't here every night, though. Chances are he's at his ranch. He owns a little spread down to the southwest of here.'

Perkins singled out the men he had in mind and the poker game got under way. Hatfield liked their looks and approved of Perkins' judgment. Digesting what he had learned, he felt that he might be able to bring some semblance of order to what unpleasantly resembled chaos with potentialities for serious trouble. He hoped so. Captain McDowell wouldn't relish having to send a troop of Rangers badly needed elsewhere to clean up the section.

The game broke up before midnight and all headed for bed, leaving their companions to collect assorted headaches at their leisure.

'But I want you all on the job an hour after sunrise,' Hatfield warned them. 'I don't want to have to come hunting for anybody.'

After looking him over, the carters decided they would not require hunting for, sleep or no sleep. Leaving tomorrow's problems till tomorrow, Hatfield went to bed blissfully unaware that more trouble was even then in the making.

CHAPTER SIX

Night brooded like a nesting bird over the wild and desolate country of the upper Big Bend. Lonely Cajun Mountain, fifteen miles south of Sanders, its slopes grown with prickly pear, *granjeño* and dagger, loomed darkly against the starry filigree of the blue-black sky. Far to the east, the Pecos River moaned and thundered in its sinister canyon under haunted cliffs.

In the shadow of Cajun Mountain the broad gray ribbon of the Chihuahua Trail—gray as the ashes of burned bones—was like the ghost of a tortured snake that writhed and contorted in silent agony.

With Cajun at their backs, perhaps a hundred yards from where the trail curved around a black boulder of cliff, a silent group of men stood in the gloom of a thicket. Behind them their patient horses bulked large in the gloom. Motionless, their tenseness accentuated by their silence, the men stood, their eyes fixed on the gray ribbon which slithered up from the southwest.

The night was deathly still, with little to blunt the sharp edge of the silence. Occasionally, a distant cow could be heard popping the bushes on the slopes below Cajun, or the weird cry of an owl would drift down from the topmost branch of a blasted piñon.

A faint breath of wind wafted up from the south, and on its invisible wings came sound. First a faint sighing like the whisper of the incoming tide. The sighing grew to the murmur of the ripple of water on a shingly beach. The murmur swelled to a mutter, deepened, acquired volume, became a grinding rumble, a monotonous jarring that quivered through the night and grew ever louder.

Somewhere an owl hooted in a kind of unnatural screaming note. The group in the thicket stirred.

'That'll be Sam,' muttered a slender, broad-shouldered man, evidently the leader of the band. 'Get set!'

A match flickered in cupped hands, lowered to the ground. There was a sputtering hiss, a spurt of sparks and a swirl of blue smoke barely visible in the starlight. The match winked out. The men stood tense and alert, staring toward the dark shoulder of cliff.

'Hope you timed it right,' muttered the leader.

'I did,' replied the man who struck the match. 'I figured it several times. Don't worry.'

Where the trail swerved around the bulge of the cliff something suddenly loomed grotesque and monstrous in the shadows. It was a ponderous freighting wagon drawn by eight straining mules. On the seats beside the driver sat an armed guard. It rumbled into the deeper shadow beneath the cliff overhang.

A second wagon appeared, a third, a fourth and a fifth. Each in turn vanished into the ebony dark beneath the overhang. The cliff towered black and menacing in the starlight.

Abruptly its mighty bulk seemed enveloped in a sheet of yellow flame. The overhang bulged outwards as from the blow of a mighty fist plunging upward from the bowels of the earth. There was shattering roar, then a mighty rumbling and crashing.

Through the thunderclap of sound came the screams of stricken mules and the yells of terrified men as the whole ponderous overhang rushed downward to rock the trail with its earthquake shock.

Lances of fire spurted from the shadowy group at the thicket edge. The staccato cracks of rifles punctuated the ghastly turmoil under the cliff. Yells of agony echoed the reports. There were a few wild answering shots from the welter of death and pain where the wagons lay crushed and broken under the fallen overhang.

Another roaring volley from the thicket, then silence save for the moaning of the crippled mules.

The band surged forward from the thicket, guns ready; but nothing menaced them from the scene of carnage at the cliff base.

Torches flickered as the drygulchers

gathered around the broken wagons. They mercifully shot several injured mules to put them out of their misery; mercy that hadn't been shown to the drivers and guards. Then they tore into the jumble of stone, tumbling the fragments aside until they could reach the wagons. They ripped open the loads, scattering them in wild confusion, uttered excited curses and gutteral exclamations of satisfaction.

A string of pack mules was led from the shelter of the deeper thicket. Quickly the rawhide *aparejos*—pack sacks—were filled to bursting with the loot.

'Hop to it!' growled the leader, glancing at the starry clock wheeling westward across the sky. 'It'll be daylight before we know it, and we've got a long ways to go.'

Ten minutes later the band rode off through the thickets, bearing away from the trail, west by north.

'A good haul this time,' one remarked. 'One of the best we've made.'

'We can't complain,' agreed the slender leader. 'Safer than running the stuff in ourselves, and all clear profit. Okay, Barnes, you take charge now. Hole up till dark. I'm riding south. Don't want to be too long, and I want to keep an eye on things. I've a notion we'll be set to do some more business before long.'

He spoke to his tall horse and a moment later vanished into the darkness. The loaded mules forged on toward the rugged hills to the west.

Back under the fallen overhang, where the rifle wagons lay, the crushed mules and the scattered dead, all was quiet save for the hollow moan of a dying man, overlooked where he lay beneath a thick bush.

CHAPTER SEVEN

The Gomez train got under way an hour after sunrise on the dot. The carts were bunched closely and Hatfield had arranged them so that American and Mexican drivers alternated. Beside each driver's knee rested a loaded rifle.

The guards, well separated, paced their horses alongside the carts.

'We're handling this train just as if it were a trail herd,' Hatfield told them. 'Point riders up toward the front, swing riders a third of the way back, flank riders another third back, and a couple of men always riding drag, a ways behind the last cart. Whenever you can, scatter out over the prairie, and never under any circumstances bunch together. If you'd been handling the chore this way the other night what happened wouldn't have happened. This way you have all the advantage on your side. A raiding bunch can't concentrate their fire, and they can't scatter like you can. There's no holing up all over the range.'

Gomez was present to see the train off. He seemed a bit bewildered at Hatfield's innovations.

'Things were not ordered thus in my grandfather's time, nor in my father's, for that matter,' he said, shaking his head. 'The guards sat in comfort beside the drivers, and seldom indeed were they needed.'

'Verily, one generation passeth away, and another cometh,' Hatfield quoted lightly. 'Times change, sir. Your granddad made out with an old Sharpe's cap-and-ball, but I notice you pack a modern Winchester in your saddle boot.'

'Aye, times change,' Gomez agreed moodily, 'and sometimes I doubt if for the better.'

'I think they do,' Hatfield replied. 'Progress is always accompanied by violence and turmoil, but in the end it pays off.'

'Perhaps,' Gomez admitted dubiously, 'but before new activities started in this section, my carts made their trips in peace.'

'I expect to see the day return when they'll make it peacefully again,' Hatfield said. 'But with things as they are at present, we must be ready for any emergency. Your train will reach Sanders all right, and without losses.'

'I hope so,' Gomex said. 'I'll admit I am worried over losses and delays. I hope you won't have any trouble in Sanders.'

'Guess I can take care of any that happens

along,' Hatfield told him. 'Be seeing you, sir.'

The carts rolled along at a steady pace, kicking up a cloud of dust, the particles dancing and glinting like sparks of burning gold in the sunlight. To right and left rolled the emerald billows of the rangeland, tipped with the amber of the ripening grass heads. The distant hills were already flecked with the bronze and scarlet of the coming autumn. Little streams etched the green robe of the prairie with silver.

Hatfield knew that the cloak of sunshine and peace could easily cover lethal intent, and took no chances. Riding in front of the train, his keen eyes constantly probed thickets, groves and rock clumps. He carefully studied the movements of birds and little animals whenever the opportunity arose.

After a while they began passing clumps of cattle wearing Gomez' Clover Leaf brand and Hatfield knew they were on his employer's range. His vigilance increased when he saw, some distance ahead, a single rider sitting a sturdy bay at the edge of the trail. At his signal the guards immediately began fanning out to menace the lone horseman from half a dozen different points. Then as they drew nearer he saw that it wasn't a horseman backing the bay, but a slender girl. She spoke to her horse and came riding to meet him. Hatfield decided she was not at all hard to look at.

She was a rather small girl with great

flashing black eyes, curly black hair cut quite short, and a graceful, nicely rounded figure. Her lips were vividly red and sweetly turned, her nose straight, with a dainty powdering of freckles on the bridge. He absently noted that they spilled over onto her creamily tanned cheeks and were, he thought, quite becoming. She wore overalls, and a rather mannishly cut blue shirt as faded as his own. It was unbuttoned at the throat and just showed the soft upper swell of her young breasts. A broad-brimmed 'J. B.,' rather battered, was perched jauntily on her black curls.

'Hello!' she greeted. 'You're Mr. Hatfield, aren't you?'

'That's right,' he agreed, somewhat surprised, 'and you?'

'I'm Patricia Gomez, mostly known as Pat, or "that darned tomboy",' she replied. 'I'm riding to Sanders with you.'

'I'm not so sure you are,' he answered. 'In the first place you haven't asked permission.'

Her round white little chin went up.

'I'm not in the habit of asking permission of someone who works for my father,' she said tartly.

Hatfield regarded her a moment, his eyes narrowing, for her tone irritated him.

'Well, you're asking this one,' he told her sternly. 'Now don't go throwing a tantrum; it won't do you a bit of good. And I'm perfectly capable of hauling you out of that hull and giving you a good spanking if you try it.'

Her reaction was surprising. For an instant she looked startled, and a bit indignant. Then suddenly she lowered her long black lashes and regarded him through their silken fringe.

'I really think I might enjoy it,' she murmured pensively. 'You have nice—hands.'

At times, even the Lone Wolf could be taken aback, and this was one of them. While he was trying to frame an appropriate reply, she burst into a merry laugh that crinkled her eyes at the corners and showed her white little teeth against her red lips.

'Please!' she said. 'I really do want to go, and I won't be a bit of trouble. Ask the boys; I've ridden with the trains before.'

Jim Hatfield proceeded to violate a cardinal rule of the Rangers. Never temporize; it's the first step toward backing down. Give your orders and make them stick!

'And if something should happen to you I'll catch merry blazes from your father,' he replied.

'Oh, no you won't,' she instantly countered. 'He gave up trying to make me behave, long ago. Please!'

'Oh, the devil! Kids could always get the best of me,' he growled resignedly.

'I'm not a kid!' she declared indignantly. 'I'm twenty-one.'

'So young?' he exclaimed with simulated surprise. 'I'd have given you twenty-five, at least.'

Miss Patricia gasped. 'Well, I—I never!' she exploded. Hatfield proceeded to pour it on.

'Of course I know appearances are deceptive, especially where the female of the species is concerned,' he conceded, 'but usually a woman tries to look younger than she actually is.'

For a moment it appeared that the tantrum was really going to take place, but she controlled her temper, not without effort.

'You look like a gentleman, but I'm beginning to have my doubts!' she snapped.

'Appearances are deceptive,' he repeated.

Then abruptly she laughed again, and Hatfield felt that laughter became her type of good looks.

'I think you're deliberately trying to get my bristles up,' she said. 'Oh, I've got my share of the famous Gomez temper, but I usually keep a tight latigo on it. I'm not going to quarrel with you, and thank you for agreeing to put up with me. I really will be good. I promise.'

'Okay, then,' he answered. 'Trot back along the line, and keep close to the carts.'

'I'd rather ride up here with you,' she demurred, pacing her horse alongside his.

'And be a prime target for a slug if some drygulcher happened to throw one this way.'

Abruptly her eyes were grave. 'Do you really think there's danger of such a thing happening?' she asked.

Hatfield shrugged his broad shoulders. 'From what I hear of the goings-on in this section of late, it wouldn't overly surprise me,' he said.

She regarded him through her lashes again. 'And,' she asked slowly, 'don't you consider that you might be a prime target up here?'

'I took that into consideration when I accepted the job,' he replied. 'That's part of what your dad pays me for.'

'Yes,' she answered, 'but I don't think it's exactly fair for an owner to allow somebody else to take risks to protect his property that he doesn't take himself; and I happen to own half of the freighting business. That was stipulated in my grandfather's will, and I came of age last month.'

Hatfield turned in the saddle to stare at her. 'Good Lord!' he exploded. 'A Lady Boss! Don't you know that's anathema in cow country?'

She gazed at him with increased interest. 'Your choice of words is rather unusual, for a cowhand,' she remarked.

'Perhaps, for a cowhand,' he admitted.

'But don't worry, I won't try to do any bossing on this trip,' she assured him. 'In fact, I've never interfered with my father's handling of the business, except to give him a little advice now and then. For example, when he came back with Mr. Conley's suggestion that he hire a competent man to handle the trains,

I urged, insisted, rather, that he do just that. I felt sure we could depend on anybody Mr. Conley sent.'

'Sorry he didn't send a gentleman?' Hatfield asked.

'Oh, stop it!' she exclaimed. 'After what you just told me I'm in no mood to indulge in persiflage. It's not pleasant to think of you risking your life this way.'

Glancing at her he saw that her red lips were quivering. Suddenly he smiled down at her.

'Another reason why I don't want you up here is that you're too darn distracting,' he said. 'I can't keep my eyes where they belong.'

She blushed a little and laughed. 'Nice of you to say it of a woman who looks half a dozen years older than she actually is.'

'Now who's indulging in persiflage! I didn't say half a dozen, only four. But I don't think we have much to worry about out here on the open range,' he reassured her. 'Be different when we get in the hills.'

'Then I can stay here?'

'For a while, anyway,' he told her. 'But keep quiet; I've got to keep a watch on things.'

They rode on in silence, while the sun climbed toward the zenith and the dark hills to the northeast drew ever nearer. At noon they halted for an hour beside a little stream to water the mules and eat. Hatfield figured that, baring accidents, they should reach Sanders shortly before nightfall. He hoped so, for he had no desire to have night catch them in the hills below where Sanders sat in its canyon mouth.

The carters appeared to take Pat Gomez' presence as a matter of course. Hatfield decided they liked her.

'She's quite a gal,' old Perkins remarked in an aside. 'A riding, shooting tomboy, but a real little lady, and purty as a spotted pony. I think she wraps old Gomez around her finger without much trouble. And between you and me I figured she's got more brains than he has. I know she's been telling him he ought to get wagons in place of the carts. With both of you working on him, maybe you can make him see daylight.'

CHAPTER EIGHT

Mid-afternoon found them rolling in the shadow of Cajun Mountain, where the trail swept around its base in a broad curve.

Suddenly Hatfield jerked Goldy to a standstill and shouted for the carts to halt. Directly ahead the trail was blocked by a wild jumble of smashed wagons, heaps of broken stone and dead mules.

Hatfield glanced back along the train and saw that the guards were obeying orders. They sat their horses tense and watchful, but they were not bunching.

'Stay here,' he told Pat and paced Goldy forward. His face was bleak, his eyes coldly gray as he viewed the scene of slaughter. Beside the hideous tangle he dismounted and inspected the wrecked wagons. He noted instantly that the loads—bales and hides and wool—had been ripped open and scattered about. He glanced around, puzzled, and saw a gleam of something bright half hidden in the dust. It was a Mexican silver dollar, brand new. Scattered about he found three more.

'So,' he mused, eyeing the coins, 'so Senor Fisher is smuggling in contraband silver. Which means he's smuggling goods back across the river. Well, that doesn't concern the Rangers. This is a Federal offense to be handled by the Customs boys, but these snake-blooded killings, they're something else again. An utterly vicious outfit is responsible for them, and they left no witnesses.'

He glanced up at the shattered cliff, moved over to its base and sniffed sharply. In an air pocket at the base the fumes of dynamite were still faintly discernible.

'Blew the cliff down on top of the train and then cut loose on the guards and drivers. Yes, utterly vicious.'

He browsed around and quickly found the thicket where the outlaws had holed up. The ground was sprinkled with exploded cartridges.

He noted that the growth was crushed and broken, with dangling branches, as if large, unwieldy objects had been forced through it. Amid the prints of horses' irons were other narrower prints.

'Pack mules,' he decided. 'They loaded up a train of mules with the silver.'

The trail left by the heavily laden mules was easy to see. It headed north by west, but it was many hours old and to follow it would be nonsense, even if he had the time. He came back to where Pat sat her horse and called to Perkins and Miguel to join him.

'You'd better come, too,' he told the girl. 'It isn't a pretty picture over there, but a lot of questions are going to be asked about this business and I want you to see what happened.'

Pat was white to the lips, but she merely nodded and followed with Perkins and Miguel.

'You'll notice these men have been dead for many hours,' Hatfield said. 'And it's plain to see how the cliff was blown down. Some of the carters were killed by falling rocks, others were shot to death.'

'But what in blazes were the hellions after?' wondered Perkins. 'Hides and wool! That stuff ain't worth stealing.'

'The wagons likely packed other goods more valuable,' Hatfield answered. 'You wouldn't find them left behind, of course.'

'Reckon that's so,' Perkins admitted

dubiously as he estimated the loads with his eyes.

Hatfield did not mention the coins he had deftly pocketed. He led his companions to the thicket and showed them where the outlaws holed up and the loaded mules took off. Then he returned to the train and beckoned one of the guards.

'Prescott, you ride back to Aguilar and notify the sheriff.' he ordered. 'Tell him what we found here and that I said it must have happened this morning sometime before daylight. All right, get the train moving. Swerve around this mess and head for Sanders; it's late.'

The train bypassed the wreckage and rolled on, the carters grim and nervous, casting apprehensive glances up the brushgrown slopes, anxiously eyeing each bend in the trail.

'See what I meant by what I said a while back?' Hatfield remarked to Pat.

She shuddered. 'It was horrible!' she said. 'Who could have done such a thing?'

'That remains to be found out,' Hatfield said quietly. He had little doubt as to who Kane Fisher would blame for the outrage. What bothered him more was the good chance that Fisher would consider retaliation in order. The threatened cart war had already passed the initial stage.

He fingered the silver coins in his pocket. Their discovery had opened up a new and ominous phase. That Fisher was indulging in a bit of smuggling was not particularly surprising. It was prevalent along the Border and afforded a chance for the unscrupulous to reap large and quick profits. Border Texans looked upon smuggling tolerantly. Many a prosperous merchant or ranch owner had gotten his start slipping contraband to and fro across the Rio Grande. Peace officers, on the other hand, were inclined to view the practice with a jaundiced eye because of the inevitable adjuncts of robbery and violence. Out-and-out owlhoots looked on the smuggler as fair game and there had been many sanguinary encounters between the two classes of law breakers.

Hatfield was convinced that the latest incident was the work of Javelina, the shadowy bandit who for some months had been operating successfully in the Border country. It had all the earmarks—savage ingenuity and utter ruthlessness. Javelina never left any witnesses.

So far so good, but the paramount question remained unanswered—who was Javelina? Hatfield had been unable to arrive at any definite conclusion relative to Sebastian Gomez. He was very much of an enigma. It seemed illogical that a man of Gomez' economic stability would resort to such practices; but Hatfield was pretty well convinced that Gomez harbored a deep resentment that was all too prevalent in men of his blood who dwelt north of the Rio Grande. Brooding over slights, injustices and discrimination could build up an obsession under the prodding of which a formerly normal mind might be turned into strange channels and enjoy a vicarious revenge from lawless acts. Hatfield had encountered similar cases. Such a condition might well be the case of Sebastian Gomez. Glancing at the sweet girl riding beside him, Hatfield reflected sadly that true it is, 'Man's inhumanity to man makes countless thousands mourn!'

Kane Fisher he had already written off as a bumbling corner-cutter who quite likely would end up a financial success and a 'pillar of society' unless somebody mowed him down before he reached the point where he would consider operating strictly inside the law to his advantage. If he really did instigate that raid on Gomez' train the other night when three men were killed, he'll get mowed down, all right, the Ranger promised himself grimly.

The trail wound on through the bleak hills. The shadows lengthened, birds called sleepily in the thickets, overhead the clouds were piled in fantastic masses, and from the west came a low mutter of thunder. The higher peaks stood out like frozen flame, bathed in the lurid glare of a monstrous sunset, their vast shoulders swathed in robes of dusky purple. And in the hollows the dark shadows of the dusk were already gathering.

Hatfield turned to Pat. 'You've been along this trail before, haven't you?' he asked.

'Yes,' she replied, 'lots of times.'

'How far are we from Sanders, would you say?'

'At least seven miles.'

Hatfield shook his head. 'We hung around that wreck too long,' he said. 'We'll never make it before dark. You stay put, I'm going to look things over.'

He wheeled his horse and rode back along the train. Beside Perkins, who was riding what would have been swing with a trail herd, he drew rein.

'Keep them close together,' he ordered. 'Each mule's nose against the tailgate of the cart ahead. I don't expect trouble, but we're taking no chances. What they saw back there under that cliff has got the boys jumpy. I don't want any pulling out sideways if something should break loose. With them bunched they'll have to keep in line. But don't let your boys bunch. Keep them apart no matter what happens. As I said, I don't expect anything, but we don't want to get caught with our cinches loose. It's what you don't expect that gives you real trouble.'

With a wave of his hand to the other guards he rode back to the head of the train.

'Looks like rain but maybe it'll pass over,' he remarked to Pat. She nodded without

74

speaking. Since the scene of horror under the cliff she had been very silent. Hatfield wondered what she was thinking about, and how much she really knew of what was going on in the section.

From the rear sounded a loud shouting. Hatfield glanced back and saw a big coach drawn by six mettlesome horses rolling swiftly past the train. Perched on the high seat beside the driver was a guard with a double-barrelled shotgun across his knees.

'The Presidio-Sanders stage,' remarked Pat. 'It's late; should have passed us an hour ago.'

On came the stage, rocking and swaying, tires grinding, springs creaking and groaning. It flashed past them in a swirl of dust, driver and guard shouting greetings.

'No passengers today,' Pat remarked. 'That's unusual. A good deal of travel from Presidio north.'

'Driver making time like he sure has places to go,' observed Hatfield. 'Look at him whiz up that slope!'

'They're supposed to make connections with the stage from Sanders to Goliad,' Pat explained. 'They transfer passengers and express at Sanders.'

Before the train reached the bottom of the long slope the stage had disappeared over its crest, with only a few dancing particles of dust to mark its passing.

With the tired mules moving at a shambling

walk, the long train crawled up the slope. When Hatfield and Pat, pacing their horses in front of the lead cart, topped the crest, the stage was nearly two miles distant, crawling up another and steeper slope.

'That sag's slowed him down a bit,' Hatfield observed. 'They—what the devil!'

The stage driver had thrown up his hands, reeled sideways and pitched from his high seat. Even before the crack of the rifle reached their ears, the guard slumped down out of sight. The stage came to a plunging halt.

From the brush that lined the trail on either side darted half a dozen figures to converge on the coach.

CHAPTER NINE

Hatfield turned in his saddle. 'Come along, fast!' he shouted to the guards and sent his great sorrel speeding down the slope.

'Trail, feller, trail!' he urged. 'All creation's busted loose over there!'

Goldy proceeded to give everything he had. He flattened his ears, blew through his nostrils and slugged his head above the bit. His steely legs shot backward like pistons, his irons drummed the hard surface as he lengthened his stride more and more. Hatfield crouched low in the hull, peering ahead, estimating the distance.

The outlaws were running back and forth between the stage and the brush, seemingly packing heavy objects. They were working fast and in perfect unison, apparently knowing just what they were about. Hatfield slid his heavy Winchester from the saddle boot. Goldy, straining every nerve, swiftly closed the distance. The rifle was sighted for a thousand yards; shooting beyond that was very much guesswork.

Fifteen hundred yards—a mile—twelve hundred yards—eleven. Hatfield raised the long gun to his shoulder.

'Steady, feller!' he called. Goldy levelled off in a smooth running walk. Hatfield's eyes glanced along the sights. He squeezed the trigger.

The rifle bucked, smoke spurted from the muzzle. Through the swirling mist Hatfield thought he saw heads duck. He lowered the muzzle a trifle, squeezed the trigger again. Swiftly as he could work the ejection lever he raked the distant group with slugs. At the fourth shot a man staggered, lurched, stumbled, then went reeling into the brush. Hatfield fired again and again, counting his shots. The last outlaw vanished into the growth. He stuffed fresh cartridges into the empty magazine and sprayed lead back and forth across the face of the brush. Slamming the empty rifle back into the saddle boot, he loosened his big Colts in their sheaths. His eyes never leaving the bristle of growth he dashed up to the stage, jerked Goldy to a halt and left the saddle while the horse was still in motion. Crouching low he dashed into the brush and stood peering and listening. He saw nothing. There was no sound save the champing and snorting of the stage horses. Gliding here and there he found where the owlhoots had tethered their horses. Bending low and examining the ground, he spotted several blood spots on the leaves.

'Nicked one of them, all right,' he muttered, 'but it's dark venous blood, not arterial. Afraid he isn't hit very hard.'

Broken branches and crushed leaves showed the course the outlaws had taken, but Hatfield regretfully shook his head. It would be black dark in another twenty minutes. Hopeless to try and follow the trail through the tangle of chaparral. He turned back to the stage.

The guard's body lay slumped between the seat and the dashboard. The driver was on his hands and knees in the trail, his bloody head weaving from side to side.

Hatfield hurried to him just as Perkins and his guards pulled their horses to a foaming halt beside the coach. Pat Gomez was with them, her face white, her eyes great dark pools of horror. But she swung to the ground and joined Hatfield beside the wounded driver.

'I've got bandages in my saddle pouches, and some salve,' she said. 'I always carry them.'

'Okay,' Hatfield nodded. 'Fetch them.' He had eased the driver to a sitting position and was examining the bleeding furrow in his scalp with sensitive fingertips.

'No sign of a fracture,' he announced. 'Can't tell about concussion. How do you feel, old timer?'

'Head hurts to beat hell and I can't seem to see good,' the old man mumbled. 'Eyes clearing up, though. Gosh! I'm covered with blood!'

'Be glad you are,' Hatfield told him. 'A freely bleeding head wound is a lot better than one that doesn't bleed. I figure you're just creased. We'll tie you up and you should be all right. Perkins, give him some water from your canteen and then let me have some to wash this gash. Okay, Pat, smear on the ointment soon as I finish, and unroll a length of bandage. Miguel, you and a couple of the boys range around a bit in the brush over there. I don't think the hellions will come back, but don't take any chances. The rest of you hightail back to the train. Keep the carts moving. We want to get out of these infernal hills as soon as we can. Wait, one of you take over the stage. We'll stow this fellow in the coach and make him comfortable. Put the guard's body in, too.

'Got anything to tell us?' he asked the driver

as he deftly rolled a cigarette and put it between his lips.

'Not much,' the old timer replied, taking deep satisfying drags. 'First thing I knew was when the sky fell on me. I don't remember anything else till I found you working over me.'

'What was the stage packing?' Hatfield asked.

'The Clayton Mine clean-up,' the driver replied. 'Nigh onto thirty thousand in gold.' He mumbled profanity.

'How in blazes the buzzards knew we were packing it is beyond me,' he said. 'Was supposed to be a dead secret. Tomorrow a wagon will roll that's supposed to pack the gold to Sanders and then on to the railroad. Seems nothing is safe nowadays.'

Hatfield nodded sober agreement. He supported the driver to the coach and made him as comfortable as the circumstances would permit. The body of the guard was placed on the floor.

Miguel and his companions returned from prowling the brush. 'It would seem they kept on going,' he said. 'We followed the trail a little way. They appear to have headed west by a little north, though of course they could turn to another direction any time. Perhaps they have a hole-up somewhere near.'

'Possibly,' Hatfield agreed, 'but there's nothing we can do about it now. Get the carts moving.'

The train rolled on again through the thickening gloom, the stage in front, the horses snorting and prancing nervously. The sky was now heavily overcast and a steely gray in color, the fires of the sunset having died to murky ash. On either side the brush grown slopes stretched upward to the rimrock over which a wan glow still played.

'See why I wasn't anxious for you to come with us?' Hatfield remarked to Pat.

'It was awful!' she replied, her lips trembling, 'but just the same I'm glad I came. I've had a first hand picture of what you men are up against.'

'Oh, I don't suppose it's always as bad as today,' Hatfield said cheerfully. 'And anyway, we didn't have to dodge any lead ourselves, which is some consolation.'

'But next time you may not be so lucky,' she replied morosely. 'I wish Captain McDowell would send some Rangers to restore order. Dad, and others, wrote him asking for help. Do you think he will send them?'

'I've a notion Captain Bill is a busy man these days,' Hatfield evaded, 'but he never lets folks down. He may move in an unexpected manner.'

'I hope so,' she sighed. 'This is getting to be terrible country and it was once so beautiful and peaceful.'

'The wheel turns,' he consoled her. 'It will be peaceful again. Cloudy and gloomy tonight, but the sun will shine tomorrow.'

'Right now I'd settle for a moon,' she said, glancing up at the darkening canopy that seemed to press down on the hilltops.

Full darkness quickly fell and the night was so black they could not see a dozen feet ahead. The grind of the tires and the plodding beat of hoofs echoed back hollowly from the slopes. A chill wind rustled leaves and branches and drew from them an eerie, heart-chilling music. A mule brayed without warning and every driver from end to end of the train jumped and swore. From the wooded depths came the mournful, hauntingly beautiful plaint of a hunting wolf.

Hatfield sensed that Pat had moved her horse closer to his. Impulsively he reached, groped in the dark and found her hand. Her fingers clung to his and they were icy cold.

'Take it easy,' he comforted. 'We'll soon be out of it.'

'This is awful dark!' she murmured. 'I imagine I see eyes staring at me, and the tree branches move and crawl like living things. Every time an owl whimpers it sounds like a lost baby crying.'

'Been a hard day on the nerves,' he replied.

'I don't think you have any,' she retorted.

'I'm just more used to such things, that's all,' he replied, 'but I could do with a little light, even a star or two. Sky's black as pitch. Anyway it isn't raining. It looked like it would be by now. A good downpour and some thunder and lightning and we might have a stampede. The mules are nervous, too, and sometimes they get scared for no reason at all.'

'I don't blame them,' she replied. 'It wouldn't take much to start me screaming. I'm not superstitious, but if there ever was a night when ghosts and goblins prowl, this is it.'

'Even a ghost couldn't see his way around tonight,' Hatfield chuckled. 'I figure they're all holed up.'

'And I wish we were,' she declared fervently. 'You're nice not to remind me I insisted on coming along. I'm ashamed of myself, giving you something more to worry about.'

'Just having you here makes up for it,' he said.

'That was nice. I feel better,' she replied. Her fingers tightened on his.

Gradually the hills fell away and the trail wound across open rangeland. Without the shadows cast by the giant slopes, it was a bit lighter. And then, in the distance ahead, they made out a faint sparkle and glow that steadily grew plainer. The lights of Sanders.

'Where you going to stay tonight?' Hatfield asked Pat as they neared the town.

'I can get a room at the Cattleman's Hotel,' she replied. 'There's a good restaurant on the ground floor. You can get a room there, too, unless you prefer to bunk at the station with the boys.'

83

'I think I'll take a chance on the hotel,' he replied. He saw her eyes glint sideways toward him, but it was too dark for him to be able to read their expression.

She was silent for a moment, then she said, 'I'll wait for you in the restaurant, after I've changed and washed up. We'll eat together. Okay?'

'Okay,' he agreed. 'Be with you soon as I get the train put away. Too late to do anything more tonight.

'But you'd better come along with me to the stage station,' he added. 'They'll want to know what happened, and we both saw it.'

CHAPTER TEN

Sanders, a cow and sheep town of the wild and woolly variety, sat in the mouth of a deep canyon, one wall of which rose over the main street. From the days of its inception it was a wild frontier town. Outlaws from the canyons and mountains of the Big Bend country made it their headquarters. It did a thriving traffic in wet cows, stolen in Mexico and driven across the Rio Grande. It was also a junction for the stage and freight lines running east and west, north and south. It had a reputation of being a salty pueblo, and lived up to it.

The usual quota of saloons lined the main

street and there were a number of large general stores, for Sanders was a supply center for an extensive cattle and mining country.

There was excitement aplenty, spiced with vivid profanity, when the stage rolled up to the station with its grisly burden. The station agent, a corpulent and worried-looking individual, outswore everybody else.

'Things are going from bad to worse all the time,' he declared. 'This is the limit! Did you get a look at any of the hellions?'

'A thousand yards was about as close as I got to them,' Hatfield replied. 'They didn't waste any time getting in the clear, and there was no following them through the brush in the dark.'

'No, I suppose not,' agreed the agent, 'and I don't suppose anybody ever will follow them. Javelina and his bunch sure as the devil, and nobody has been able to track him down.'

'You better send somebody to meet the sheriff,' Hatfield suggested. 'He'll be headed this way in the morning, anyhow.'

'Why?' asked the agent.

Hatfield told him of the raid on Kane Fisher's wagon train. The agent swore some more.

'You fellers were lucky to get through,' he said, 'but I suppose the mangy coyotes were too busy with other things to pay you any mind. Chances are they'll be laying for you on the way back to Aguilar.'

'I hope so,' Hatfield said quietly.

The agent stared at him but decided not to ask any questions. He wouldn't have gotten an answer if he had.

The driver, who insisted he was okay again and fit as a fiddle, was nevertheless hustled off to a doctor. An undertaker was summoned to take charge of the guard's body.

'That feller's getting rich, I mean the undertaker,' growled the agent. 'The doctor ain't doing so bad, but the undertaker is the bully boy with a glass eye in this town.'

Across the street front the stage station was the Cattleman's Hotel, a rambling two-story structure.

'You might as well go ahead and get a room,' Hatfield told Pat. 'I'll take care of your horse.'

'Shall I get one for you, too?' she asked. 'The town looks busy tonight and there might be a shortage of accomodations.'

'Okay, if you aren't afraid you'll lift some eyebrows,' he agreed.

'I'll risk it,' she replied with a giggle. 'Let me have my saddle pouches. A girl can't travel light as a man does.'

'I usually pack a clean shirt in mine,' Hatfield said as he undid the buckles to free the pouches.

'That's enough for a man, but a girl needs something else beside overalls when she sits down to dinner with somebody.'

'You look all right in overalls,' he said, 'but

if you'd rather eat dinner without them—'

'That would cause raised eyebrows,' she said as she grabbed the pouches and whisked across the street.

'Now what the devil did she mean by that?' he wondered and turned to start the train moving.

The Sanders freight station with its barns and corral was similar to the one at Aguilar only somewhat larger. While the carts were being run into the corral and the mules stabled, Hatfield conferred with the manager.

'Mighty glad to see you,' the manager said as he checked the lists Hatfield gave him. 'I was getting worried. We'll start delivering first thing in the morning. I suppose you'll want to personally interview the consignees?'

Hatfield nodded and waited for the other to proceed.

'The chances are you'll get some complaints,' the manager predicted gloomily. 'A good deal of this stuff should have been here two days ago. When we hold up delivery, it holds up others. Better see Clem Haskins first. He owns the big new place a few doors below the Cattleman's Hotel and he's been growling the loudest. Kane Fisher has been servicing him some, but Fisher hasn't been doing so well either of late. Anything I can do for you, Mr. Hatfield?'

'Some soap and water wouldn't go bad,' Hatfield replied.

'Come right along,' said the manager. 'I've got everything you need. Going to sleep here tonight?'

'I'm staying at the hotel,' Hatfield replied. 'I suppose most of the boys hang out here?'

'That's right,' answered the manager. 'Rooms fitted up on the second floor. Most of 'em don't use them, though. They spend the night raising hell.'

'Let 'em,' Hatfield said, 'seeing as they won't have to hit the trail tomorrow.'

'No, it'll take all of tomorrow and maybe part of the day after to make deliveries and pack the loads for the return trip.'

After making sure that Goldy was properly cared for, Hatfield walked back to the business section with old Perkins. The street they followed was dark and quiet and shaded by old trees, but from the distance came the hum and mutter of Sanders' busy night life.

'She's a ripsnorter, all right,' said Perkins. 'Never stops, day or night. Always something going on and always folks coming and going. By the way, do you think that agent feller was right when he figured Javelina pulled that job on the stage today?'

'Could be,' Hatfield admitted, 'But there's no guarantee that it was. When a jigger like Javelina starts operating in a section and builds up a reputation he gets blamed for everything that happens, which plays right into the hands of any brush popping outfit that sets

88

up in business. Everybody has an eye out for Javelina and overlooks a local bunch that may be working right under their noses.'

'I've a notion you've got something there,' Perkins agreed. 'One thing's sure for certain, somebody was able to get the lowdown on just when that gold shipment would move and how.'

'You know who owns that mine?' Hatfield asked.

'It's a company,' Perkins returned. 'Gomez owns a share, and I believe Steve Ennis does, too, and one or two others in Aguilar. A good holding, all right. Nothing to set the courthouse on fire, but it makes money, or did. If they keep on losing shipments like the one today they'll be on the wrong side of the corral fence.'

Hatfield nodded thoughtfully, his black brows drawing together.

'Well, I'm going down to the Alhambra on the next corner for something to eat and a few drinks,' Perkins announced as they paused in front of the hotel. 'It's about the safest place in town, seldom more than one or two killings a night. If you'd care to drop in later, I'll be there.'

'Wouldn't be surprised if I do,' Hatfield replied. 'Be seeing you.'

He found Pat already seated at a table in the restaurant. Instead of overalls and a mannish shirt, she wore a simple, but very becoming dress. Hatfield thought she looked even more charming than before, and told her so.

'It's all wrinkled from being bundled in the pouch,' she said, giving the garment a disapproving glance, 'but anyway it makes me look like a woman instead of a tomboy.'

'I don't think anybody would mistake you for a man, even in overalls,' he smiled. 'Nature took care of that.'

'I suppose so,' she admitted, with another downward glance. 'But sit down; I thought you'd never get here. I'm starved! Oh, yes, I got us rooms, adjoining ones.'

'With a door between?' he asked.

'Really, I—I didn't notice,' she replied with a giggle and a quick look at him through her lashes.

They had a very pleasant dinner. With the elasticity of youth and perfect health, both had thrown off the anxieties of the day and were in excellent spirits. By common consent none of the grim happenings of a few hours before were discussed, nor the possibilities of what the morrow might bring forth. Their conversation consisted of banter and small talk liberally interspersed with gay laughter.

'Mind if I smoke?' Hatfield asked as he pushed back his plate.

'Not at all,' she assured him. 'I do myself sometimes, in private. I'm of Mexican descent, you know, and nearly all Mexican women smoke.'

Before he finished his cigarette, however, she stifled a yawn, very prettily, he thought.

'It's not you,' she said. 'I'm just tired. Mind if I trot upstairs? A girl can't keep on going forever like a man, you know.'

'That depends,' he replied, and got another look through her lashes.

He accompanied her to the stairs that rose from the little cubbyhole of a lobby. There was a mocking gleam in her big eyes when she said good night.

Leaving the hotel, Hatfield sauntered down the street to the Alhambra, a big, garishly lit saloon full of noise and smoke. He found Perkins and several of his guards busily reducing the stock of alcoholic beverages. They welcomed a helping hand with exuberance.

'In thish place they give you a free snake with every third drink,' Perkins said, eyeing his brimming glass with owlish gravity. 'I already done corralled two rattlers and a hognose. Aims to trade 'em all in on a boa constrictor before the night's over. Have another shnake, I mean another drink, Jim!'

Hatfield spent some time with the convivial bunch and then said good night despite their protests. Returning to the hotel, he climbed the stairs to his room and lit the lamp. He removed his hat and glanced around.

The furnishings consisted of a single chair

and a bed, but the bed was wide and looked comfortable, and outside the open window was a large tree where tree toads tinkled musically. He was rolling a cigarette when he heard a light tapping.

'Jim,' came a muffled voice, 'there is a door.'

'So I noticed when I came in,' he replied.

'And the key's on my side.'

'You're lucky.'

'Oh, I don't know!'

There was a click, the door swung wide open and Pat stepped from her darkened room into his.

She wore a robe of some soft, clinging material that molded itself perfectly to the sweet contours of her figure, her curly hair was charmingly tousled and her great eyes were slumbrous. Hatfield whistled under his breath at the picture she made.

'I waited up for you,' she said. 'Or, rather, I drowsed with one eye open and listened for you to come in. I want to talk to you.'

She sat down in the single chair, crossed her knees and regarded him intently. Hatfield sat down on the edge of the bed and finished rolling his cigarette.

'Jim,' she said, 'who the devil and what the devil are you?'

'You know my name, and I'm your dad's carting foreman,' he replied.

'Oh, sure!' she scoffed. 'You're no more a

carting foreman than I am. You may have been a cowhand, but it's been quite a while since you twirled a rope or used a branding iron. Your hands show that.'

'Good eyes,' he commented.

'You're here for some set purpose, and it isn't to manage a carting train.'

Hatfield sat silent, listening to the tree toads behind him. She proceeded to give him a real jolt.

'Jim,' she said, 'I know the talk that's going around, that my father is Javelina, the bandit leader. He isn't. If he was, I'd know it. The poor old dear couldn't harm a fly. He's so honest it hurts, and ethical to the point of eccentricity. A knight in shining armor if there ever was one. The trouble with him is that he's fifty years behind the times. He lives in the past, or what he imagines the past was and very likely wasn't. He's a chivalrous gentleman of the old school, to borrow a worn out and doubtless deceptive expression. He'd be utterly horrified if he knew I was here in your room at this time of night, wearing a robe you can see through without a bit of trouble, if you look hard enough.'

Hatfield looked, and decided not to argue the point. He was having enough trouble trying to assemble his thoughts into coherent order.

Suddenly she smiled, a smile that considerably like an impish grin.

'I was just wondering,' she said, 'what you

think of me.'

'I think,' he said slowly, 'that you have brains as well as looks.'

'The one granted, the other depends on who's looking at me,' she replied.

Hatfield reserved opinion. 'Have you any idea who started the talk about your father?' he asked.

She shook her head. 'No, it just seemed to happen and grow, like a mushroom in the dark. Steve Ennis was the first to tell me of it. He came over to our place one evening—he drops in quite often—and he was worried. He'd overheard the matter discussed in his saloon. He asked me not to tell Dad, for, as he said, it was just one of those "they say" things with nothing so far as he was able to learn to supply any basis for it.'

'Do you think your father knows about the talk?'

'I'm not sure,' she replied. 'He keeps things to himself. Of course I know he would have no trouble disproving such a ridiculous charge if it were ever made against him.'

'Doubtless, in a court of law,' Hatfield admitted, 'but unfortunately in this section of the country folks sometimes take the law into their own hands. I'm not going to belittle the seriousness of the matter. For instance, if those people over at the stage station were really convinced somebody was Javelina they might be inclined to act—impulsively.'

'I know it,' she said, 'and I'm terribly worried for Dad.' Her lips trembled, her eyes were misty.

Suddenly she locked her gaze with his. 'Jim,' she said, 'I'm going to ask you one question— are you here to try and straighten things out?'

Hatfield felt he was making no mistake in his simple answer, 'Yes.'

She drew a deep breath. 'That's all I want to know,' she said. 'I'm not asking for any particulars. And somehow, for the first time in months, I feel safe.'

She stood up, close beside him, and it seemed only natural that his arms should go around her slender waist. She swayed toward him, then gave a little gasp.

'Good heavens! The window's wide open!' she exclaimed. With a swift, graceful movement she turned and blew out the lamp.

Outside the window, the little tree toads were suddenly silent. It was quite a while before they resumed their musical tinkling.

CHAPTER ELEVEN

'Pat, I want you to do something for me,' Hatfield said as they ate breakfast together.

'Anything I can, dear,' she instantly promised.

'When we get back to Aguilar, I want you to

95

try and dig up a list of the board of directors of the Clayton Mine that lost the gold shipment yesterday. Think you can do it?'

'I'm sure I can,' she replied. 'Dad owns stock in that mine; he'll know who they are.'

'And keep it under that curly hair,' he cautioned. 'It'll be another secret between us. What are you blushing for?'

'I think any girl with a memory would blush, under the circumstances,' she said. 'Oh, stop laughing at me!'

Hatfield's first chore for the day was to visit Clem Haskins, the owner of the big new store on Main Street, where the station manager said he might expect trouble.

Haskins proved to be a lean bony man with a sallow complexion, shrewd, deep-set eyes and a tight mouth. Hatfield instantly set him down as a cold proposition. He was in anything but a pleasant mood.

'I'm just about fed up with Gomez and Fisher both,' he declared. 'This darned feuding is causing trouble for everybody. I've got half a dozen wagons waiting for stuff that should have been here forty-eight hours ago. That costs money and makes for trouble with the consignees. If this keeps up we're going to lose all our Santiago and Del Norte business to Marathon. They've got a lot longer run up from the south, but they do manage to get their trains through on time. Things are getting worse all the time, and I'm just about ready to do something about it.'

Hatfield did not ask him what he proposed to do, feeling that doubtless he wouldn't get an answer, and Haskins did not see fit to amplify his remark.

'I think you can depend on getting your shipments when promised from now on,' he assured the storekeeper.

'I hope so,' Haskins replied, not looking particularly convinced.

'Got something for us going south?' the Ranger asked.

'Yes, I've got a big shipment that'll be ready to roll tomorrow, if you can wait for it,' Haskins said. 'I can't get it ready today. It's heavy stuff, mostly machinery, and I'm shorthanded.'

'We'll wait,' Hatfield said. 'I doubt if we can finish up our chores today, anyhow.'

'Okay,' nodded Haskins. 'Have your carts in front of my place before noon; I'll want about a dozen. I don't see why the hell Gomez doesn't get rid of those dinky contraptions and use wagons.'

'Perhaps he will, in time,' Hatfield predicted. He said good day to the storekeeper and left the establishment, pondering Haskins' attitude. It seemed to Hatfield that his irritation over the delayed shipments was a bit forced.

There was a derisive gleam in the storekeeper's eyes as Hatfield walked out, his thin lips twisted crookedly in what was perhaps intended for a smile, or a sneer. As soon as he was sure Hatfield had departed and was not coming back, he hurried to a rear room.

'Okay,' he said to a man who sat there smoking a cigarette. 'Hightail and tell the boss the big buzzard is going to stay in town tonight. Now's his chance to get rid of him once and for all. He'd better. I don't like that jigger's looks one little bit. Be a hell of a note, to have our big thing tangled up at this stage of the game.'

'Right,' the other agreed laconically and slid out a door that opened onto an alley.

Hatfield visited other storekeepers and shippers and from each received a reception somewhat similar to that accorded him by Haskins. They were not so outspoken in their protests but were plainly not at all pleased with the inconveniences caused by the delay.

Last of all he visited Tom Conley's establishment. Conley was a scholarly looking old gentleman with a scanty white beard and mild blue eyes behind steel-rimmed spectacles. Deceptively mild, Hatfield felt.

'So you're Hatfield, eh?' he said when the Lone Wolf introduced himself. 'McDowell had considerable to say about you. Seems to think you'll be able to straighten out everything, singlehanded. Hope he's right. I expect to see him in a few days. Well, what have you learned?'

Hatfield told him everything that had happened, in detail. Conley listened in silence wagging his goat-like beard from time to time.

'Well,' he said, after Hatfield finished, 'well, on the surface it looks like Kane Fisher is the deep-dyed villain of the piece and Sebastian Gomez the innocent victim of his machinations.'

'Yes, on the surface,' Hatfield agreed.

Conley wagged his beard. 'I am inclined to paraphrase the Immortal Bard of Avon and say, "A pest on both their houses!"' he declared. 'That is,' he added shrewdly, 'if they're really responsible for what's going on and not somebody who's horning in on the game and taking advantage of their enmity for each other. What do you think?'

'I'm not prepared to give an answer to that just yet,' Hatfield replied, 'but it's a possibility that must not be overlooked. You've heard the talk that Gomez is Javelina?'

'Oh, sure,' Conley replied. 'Seems everybody has heard it, and nobody knows where it started or why. What do you think?'

Hatfield hesitated. Despite Pat's undoubted belief in her father's innocence, he had not yet made up his mind concerning Gomez. After all, if there was another side to him, he would not be likely to reveal it to his daughter. He answered Conley's question indirectly.

'So far as I can learn, there is no proof that he is, and for that matter, no proof that he isn't.'

'Sometimes I wonder if there really is a Javelina,' remarked Conley. 'Folks get funny notions when things are going on in a section and are inclined to blame them on some mythical character with Robin Hood or Black Bart characteristics that they invent in their own minds.'

'Whether there is or isn't a man called Javelina isn't important,' Hatfield answered. 'The fact remains that there is a shrewd, salty and utterly vicious outfit operating in this section. There's somebody at the head of it, somebody with brains. My chore, in addition to trying to prevent a real thundering cart war busting loose all over the range, is to find out who the hellion is and drop a loop on him.'

Conley nodded agreement. 'Somebody's sure raising hell hereabouts of late and shoving a chunk under a corner,' he grumbled. 'Okay, I'll have some southbound loads ready for you when you deliver my stuff; and good hunting!'

Hatfield was at the corral, supervising the packing of some southbound loads, when word was brought that the sheriff was at the stage station and wanted to see him. Leaving Perkins to finish the job, he went to the station and found the sheriff accompanied by a couple of deputies and Kane Fisher who looked to be in a very bad temper indeed.

'Well, it 'pears you're getting to be a regular customer at inquests,' the sheriff greeted him.

'But I'm of a notion you're a bad luck piece. Everywhere you show up somebody gets killed.'

'The trouble so far has been that I haven't showed up soon enough,' Hatfield replied with a significance that was perhaps lost on the sheriff.

'Well, I want you to tell me first-hand just what happened there on the trail,' the sheriff said. 'You say you didn't get a look at any of those hellions?'

'That's right,' Hatfield replied.

'And you figure you nicked one of them?'

'I found blood spots, which makes it look that way, unless the jigger got mad and bit himself,' Hatfield explained.

'You're always making bad jokes at the wrong time,' snorted Thomas. 'Why can't you be serious about serious matters? Which way did the lizards head when they went through the brush?'

'West by a little north, so far as we were able to follow the trail,' Hatfield answered. 'Was getting too dark to follow it any farther. By the way, I suppose you stopped by Fisher's wrecked wagons. You might have noticed that the trail away from there also headed west by a bit north. Might not mean anything, but then again it might.'

'You mean you figure the same outfit pulled both jobs?'

Hatfield answered the sheriff, but his eyes

were on Kane Fisher's face when he spoke.

'I'm not able to say, but there was a similarity of method that is interesting. And there's one thing I want to bring out: it's fairly conclusive that Gomez' carters couldn't have had anything to do with the wrecking of Fisher's wagons, seeing as they were all in Aguilar, as everybody knows, when the job was pulled. Just want to make it clear it couldn't have been an even-up chore for what happened to Gomez' carts on the Chihuahua Trail just this side of Aguilar the other night.'

'Who the hell said I had anything to do with that?' bawled Fisher.

'Nobody,' Hatfield instantly countered, 'but there's no use beating around the bush. You have blamed Gomez for what has happened to your wagons, and his men have blamed you for what has happened to his carts. Who's right and who's wrong will come out in the wash. I just want to set the record straight on that last job.'

Fisher mouthed and sputtered, but the sheriff said, 'What Hatfield says makes sense, Kane. The carters couldn't have had anything to do with it.'

'I ain't saying they did, but somebody wrecked my wagons and killed my drivers. I want to know who.'

'So do I,' said the sheriff, 'but so far I ain't had any luck finding out. Well, there's no sense in arguing about it all day. I'm going over to the hotel to talk to Pat Gomez. I'll want her testimony at the inquest, seeing as she saw everything, too. Come on, boys.'

He departed with his deputies. Kane Fisher lingered behind. Hatfield walked over to him.

'Well, what do *you* want?' Fisher demanded truculently.

'Just want to give you something,' Hatfield replied. 'Here!'

He thrust out his hand quickly. Fisher mechanically took what he proffered. His jaw sagged, his eyes goggled.

'Fisher, I figure it would be a good notion not to meddle with Gomez' trains in the future, don't you?' Hatfield said and turned his back and walked out.

Fisher, gripping the silver dollar, glared after him, his face a mixture of rage, bewilderment and fright.

CHAPTER TWELVE

Hatfield chuckled as he walked back to the freight station. He had thrown a scare into Fisher and might very well have made a move that would serve to at least postpone the threatened cart war. There was a chance that Fisher would lay off Gomez' trains, for a while, anyhow, for fear of reprisals he wouldn't be prepared to face. This had the inestimable value of giving individual tempers a chance to cool. Also, if the impetuous freighter was mixed up in something more serious than a little respectable smuggling, he could very well go off half-cocked and tip his hand. Hatfield felt he could follow Fisher's reasoning. He, Hatfield, was a quick-draw gunslinger whose gun was for sale. He had been brought in by Gomez to do his fighting. Somehow, he had caught onto Fisher's smuggling operations. His next logical move would be in the nature of genteel blackmail. Having Fisher over a barrel, so to say, and in a position to vigorously apply the shingle, he could demand to be cut in on the profits of the smuggling operation, which was the usual procedure of his kind. Fisher wouldn't like it, and it was reasonable to assume that he would consider Hatfield's elimination the only possible way out of his predicament. He would probably act accordingly.

Hatfield knew well he was seriously jeopardizing his own personal safety, but he was prepared to risk being eliminated if by so doing he could accomplish his objective. He was not particularly concerned over what Fisher might try to do. He would doubtless move with all the grace and finesse of a charging shorthorn on the prod.

But, as usual, there was a loose thread dangling—the shadowy and mysterious personage known as Javelina. Whoever

Javelina might be, Hatfield felt that he was something to reckon with.

Perkins dropped in and gave the Ranger a curious glance.

'Jim,' he asked, 'what the devil did you do to Kane Fisher? I passed him on the street a minute ago and he looked like he'd just seen a ghost.'

'Maybe his conscience is bothering him,' Hatfield smiled.

'Uh-huh, and if he knew what he's up against, I reckon it would bother him a blamed sight more,' Perkins predicted.

'Now what do you mean by that?' Hatfield asked.

But Perkins only grinned and left the room.

Hatfield worked until late in the closely shuttered office of the station, tabulating long lists of goods, their destination and consignees. Around midnight the station manager, who was helping, began to yawn.

'You might as well hit the hay,' Hatfield told him. 'I have only a couple more lists left to check. I won't need you any longer.'

The sleepy manager gratefully tumbled off to bed. Hatfield worked for half an hour longer, then stood up to ease his cramped legs. He shuffled the papers together, placed them in their proper order and decided to call it a night.

He blew out the lamp before opening the door, and when he stepped out onto the little porch that fronted the building, he instinctively glanced keenly about.

Everything was quiet and there was nobody in sight. He started down the steps, and took a glorious header over a rope that had been stretched just above the second one. He hit the ground with stunning force and before he could make a move, three men swarmed out of the shadows and hurled themselves upon him. Although dazed by the fall, he fought furiously, but a pistol barrel crunched against his skull and he went limp.

His attackers rose to their feet, one swearing viciously and rubbing a swelling jaw. At a word of command from another he hurried off into the darkness, still caressing the spot where Hatfield's fist had landed. A few minutes later he returned with four saddled and bridled horses.

'All right, up with him,' ordered the spokesman for the trio. 'Slim, you and Butch hold him in the hull; we'll tie him later. Get a move on before somebody comes along. If anybody tries to stop us, don't argue—shoot!'

'I don't see why we can't shoot the sidewinder right now and get it over with,' growled the man with the bruised jaw. 'What's the sense in packing him off?'

'Orders are orders,' returned the first speaker, 'and a jigger who doesn't do what the Boss tells him, just like he tells it, is in for trouble. Besides, we don't want any noise of shooting if we can help it. Those carters sleep near here and some of them might be around. All right, get going!'

CHAPTER THIRTEEN

When Hatfield recovered consciousness he gradually realized he was roped fast to the saddle of a speeding horse and slumped forward in a painfully uncomfortable position, his face buried in the animal's coarse mane. His head was one vast ache, his stomach a crawling horror. He tried to raise his head and a wave of nausea quickened the crawl and added to the horror. He slumped forward again with a gasp and fought to overcome the cloying sickness. Gradually his mind cleared a little, his head stopped spinning and he was able to take stock of his surroundings. Opening his eyes in spite of the pain involved, he slanted a glance sideways.

A man rode on either side of him. Slightly in front was a third who held the bridle of his horse. They were but blurred shadows in the faint starlight.

Despite the discomforts of his position, Hatfield decided to remain as he was for a while, in the hope that his captors might indulge in conversation. However, they rode without speaking except for an occasional muttered curse at the darkness or the roughness of the road.

Hatfield's strength was returning, accompanied by an active interest in things. Inside he was fuming. He had been caught settin', and by a mangy old trick.

'No wonder that bust on the head didn't kill me,' he muttered to himself, 'nothing inside it but hot air. Of all the dumb shorthorns, I take the blue ribbon! Wonder where this bunch is taking me, and why?'

By the position of his saddle, he knew they were climbing a fairly steep slope. On either side of the track was the thick shadow of encroaching growth with the trail, such as it was, winding snakily between. He hadn't the slightest notion where he was nor in what direction he was going. Well, it didn't particularly matter. He had a fairly good idea where the journey would end, if he didn't get some kind of a break and soon. His captors certainly hadn't dropped a loop on him just for the fun of it. It began to look like Kane Fisher might be a trifle smarter and more ruthless than he had given him credit for. That is if Fisher was responsible for what had happened. If he wasn't, who was?

Hatfield decided he had endured the discomfort of his awkward position long enough. His captors weren't doing any talking. He moved his head from side to side, groaned loudly and lurched erect, weaving from side to side to simulate returning consciousness. He hoped to give the impression that he was in much worse shape than he really was.

The lead man turned in his saddle and peered through the gloom. 'Coming out of it, eh?' he remarked in gruff tones. 'Okay, just take it easy and don't try anything or we'll have to put you back to sleep.'

'What's this all about and where are you taking me?' Hatfield mumbled dazedly.

'You'll find out,' the other replied. 'You just fork that bull and keep a latigo on your jaw. Butch, you and Slim close up on him.'

The two side riders moved their horses closer. Hatfield couldn't make much of them because of the dark, but one seemed squat and broad, the other slight of build. The man in front was taller than either.

For an hour or more they followed the rocky trail that climbed slopes, dipped into hollows and ran between wooded slopes, always with a slight increase in elevation. Hatfield surmised that it must run through the hills west of Sanders.

Abruptly the lead man swung to the left, jerking Hatfield's horse after him. The others took the same course. Brush crackled, leaves and twigs raked the Ranger's face. Then the way opened up again and the horses' irons thudded on grass covered ground. Another five minutes of slow going and a little clearing opened up. In the dim glow of the starlight

Hatfield could see the bulk of a roughly built cabin, doubtless once the home of a wandering prospector. He knew these hills were dotted with them.

In front of the closed door his captors dismounted. The lashing that bound his ankles to the stirrup straps were loosed.

'All right, unfork,' said the tall man. Hatfield did so, awkwardly. He weaved on his feet, stumbled when they touched the ground. The bulky man seized his elbow in a powerful grip. Hatfield leaned heavily against his support and when he was shoved toward the door of the cabin, which the tall man had opened, he slumped and dragged his feet. In reality, his physical condition had just about returned to normal, and his mind was functioning clearly again.

A light flared up inside the cabin. Hatfield was shoved through the door.

The single room was outfitted with a table constructed of thick planks, several rude chairs, a bunk built against one wall and a rusty iron stove. An open door showed another room with more bunks built against the walls. A rough ladder led to a trap door in the ceiling. On shelves were stores of staple provisions. Cooking utensils hung from pegs driven in the logs. Altogether quite a snug hideout that showed signs of considerable occupancy.

'Sit down there and put your hands on the

110

table,' said the tall man, gesturing to one of the chairs. Hatfield obeyed without question. He had already ascertained that his cartridge belts and guns had been removed.

The stocky man was at the moment examining his guns. 'Good irons,' he announced. 'I can use 'em.'

'No you don't,' the tall leader instantly disagreed. 'Guns like those attract attention and are remembered. A gent wearing 'em might be called on to explain where he got 'em, Butch. You hang those belts on that peg over there and leave 'em alone.'

Butch growled, but did as he was told.

'Sit down in that chair on the other side of the table and keep your gun on this gent,' the leader said. 'Slim, you keep an eye on him, too. Don't take no chances; he's bad. I'm going to fetch the Boss. He has some questions to ask high-pockets before he—takes care of him. I'd ought to be back in a couple of hours, or less.'

He paused to roll a cigarette before leaving. Hatfield slumped forward listlessly in the chair, his hands jerking on the table top, got a good look at him. He was lean, cadaverous with a long, pointed nose, a thin slit of a mouth and a cast in one eye. He looked vicious, and intelligent. He reminded Hatfield of Haskins, the Sanders storekeeper, only taller.

Of the other two, Butch was squat and powerfully built. He had a fat face and muddy eyes. Slim was scrawny, weasel faced and bright eyed. Hatfield decided he was the more dangerous of the two. His mind was more alert and his reflexes would be speedier.

The tall leader lighted his cigarette, nodded and walked out, closing the door behind him. Hatfield heard a horse's irons fade away in the distance.

Slim had squatted on the edge of the bunk that faced Hatfield. Butch sat stolidly in his chair, a gun in his thick-fingered hand. He regarded Hatfield gloomily.

Hatfield knew he was in a bad spot. He figured that unless he managed to do something about it, he didn't have long to live. When the Boss, whoever he was, arrived, he was to be asked some questions and then 'taken care of.' He suffered no illusions as to what being 'taken care of' meant.

But what could he do? Butch sat stolid and watchful, fingering his gun. Slim lounged comfortably but was equally watchful. Hatfield noted that his right hand was never far from his holster. Under present conditions, to make a move was tantamount to committing suicide. His mind worked furiously, discarding plan after plan as unpractical. The minutes flitted past and he knew his time must be getting short. He relaxed a little. He could only hope for some kind of a break and instantly take advantage of it when, and if, it came. He continued to pretend exhaustion and nervousness, his fingers twitching, his nails raking the rough wood of the table. Slim noticed.

'Feller's got the shakes,' he commented. 'Well, I don't wonder. I'd have 'em, too, if I was in his boots and waiting for the Boss. The Boss don't take kind to folks horning into his business.'

Hatfield blinked his eyes and twitched his mouth. Slim grinned evilly, evidently enjoying the contortions of his victim. He rolled a cigarette and drew in deep lungfuls of smoke, still eyeing Hatfield with malicious pleasure.

Butch sniffed the smoke, grumbled something under his breath and fished the makin's from his shirt pocket with his left hand, and deftly rolled a cigarette with the one hand. He snapped a match with his thumbnail and lighted it.

Hatfield had a sudden inspiration. He eyed the cigarette hungrily, his hands twitching.

'How about letting me have one, feller?' he said thickly.

Butch hesitated, but Slim spoke from the bunk. 'Aw, let him have one. He looks like he needs it. Don't want him going loco before the Boss gets here. Roll him one.'

Butch grunted again and proceeded to do so. 'Don't you reach for it,' he warned Hatfield. 'Keep your hands right where they are.' He leaned forward a little and placed the cigarette between the captive's lips. Hatfield kept his hands where they were—right where he wanted them to be, with his thumbs hooked under the edge of the table. Butch snapped another match and held it to the tip of the cigarette. Hatfield drew back a trifle, as if away from the heat of the flame, and Butch had to lean forward a little more. The table edge was pressed against his short ribs.

With every ounce of his strength, Hatfield shoved the table, Butch's breath exhaled in a gigantic whoosh as the edge slammed his middle. He went over backward, chair and all, his gun clattering to the floor. Slim, paralyzed by the unexpectedness of the attack, delayed a fatal second before going for his gun.

Hatfield sprang over the table in a streaking dive and grabbed Butch by the throat as he came off the floor, gasping and cursing. They grappled fiercely, reeling back and forth while Slim, dancing and yelling, tried to get in a shot. He lined his barrel but as he pulled trigger, Hatfield swung Butch's bulky form between him and the black muzzle.

Butch screamed as the heavy slug tore through his body and burned a scorching streak along Hatfield's ribs. He sagged, his knees buckling. Slim fired again and scored a clean miss. Hatfield hurled the dying man at him and dived for the fallen gun. A slug knocked splinters in his face, but he got it. Whirling around he fired point-blank at the outlaw.

Slim reeled back as if struck by a giant fist.

Hatfield kept shooting as fast as he could pull trigger. Slim had four bullets through him when he hit the floor.

Gasping, trembling, his head spinning, Hatfield sagged against the wall, clutching the rough logs for support until the room stopped whirling around and he got some air back into his laboring lungs. Then he took stock of the situation.

Slim was dead, Butch unconscious and going fast. Hatfield tossed the empty gun aside and buckled on his own sixes. He made sure the big Colts were fully loaded and felt better. He examined his bullet skinned ribs and decided that while painful, the wound was of little significance; the bleeding had already almost stopped.

His head was aching terrifically again and he was sick and weak. He would have liked to examine the cabin and its contents, but knew he must get in the clear without delay. He had no idea how much time had passed since the tall leader left or how long it would be before he got back with the Boss and perhaps others. Hatfield knew he was in no shape to give battle to one man, let alone several. He stepped over Slim's body and out the door. Beside the cabin was a leanto under which the horses were tethered. He managed to fumble one loose in the dark and after a couple of tries got into the saddle. He turned the horse's head away from the cabin and gave it a free rein. Direction didn't matter, just so he put distance between himself and the clearing.

The horse forced his way through the brush and eventually came out onto a semblance of a trail. Hatfield quickened his pace and rode steadily for several miles, lurching and swaying in the saddle, his condition not improving. Finally, when the frightful pound at his temples and the increasing nausea became unbearable, he turned the animal from the trail and rode into the growth. Ahead he could hear a musical tinkle of water and he felt that nothing in the world was so desirable as a long drink. The cayuse halted of his own accord on the bank of a little brook. Hatfield slid from the saddle and drank and drank. Then he lurched away from the stream a few yards, into the heart of a thicket, and sank to the ground to lie with his face buried in the soft carpet of the fallen leaves.

The sun was shining when he awoke from his sodden sleep of utter exhaustion. He was stiff and sore, but the headache was gone and his stomach felt normal again though decidedly empty. He wormed his way out of the thicket and looked around.

The horse had not strayed and was cropping grass by the stream. He removed the bit and allowed it to eat a while longer while he smoked a cigarette. After bathing his face in the cool water he mounted and rode away from the brook to shortly regain the trail, which was little more than a game track. Whether it was the one by which he was taken to the cabin he had no way of telling although he thought it very likely was; but he was fairly certain that Sanders lay somewhere to the east. He turned the horse's head toward the sun and rode on. An hour later, on reaching the crest of a rise, he saw a smudge of smoke that he knew must mark the site of the town. Another hour and he was riding through the outskirts.

Old Perkins was standing on the porch and looking decidedly worried when Hatfield pulled up in front of the station. He let out a joyous whoop.

'Where in hell have you been?' he demanded. 'You look like you made a night of it. We found your hat beside the steps and knew something must have happened, but didn't know what to do about it. Decided we'd best wait and see if you'd show up. What did happen?'

'I'll tell you all about it later,' Hatfield promised as he dismounted. 'How's the work going?'

'Just finished loading the last cart,' said Perkins, adding doubtfully, 'figure to roll 'em today?'

'We'll see,' Hatfield replied. 'Right now, I'm going over to the hotel for something to eat. I'm starved. Look after the cayuse, will you?'

'Sure,' Perkins agreed. 'And you'd better see

Miss Pat right away and tell her you're all right. She's about half loco, take it from me.'

The door between stood open when Hatfield entered his room. Pat came running to him.

'Good heavens, Jim! What happened to you?' she cried. 'You look terrible!'

She clung to him, her breath coming in sobs. 'When you didn't show up last night I was scared stiff,' she said. 'Then I decided that maybe you'd gotten into an all night poker game. But when morning came and there was still no sign of you, and nobody had any notion what had become of you, I thought I'd go crazy. What did happen?'

He dropped wearily into a chair and briefly recounted the night's experiences. 'Now I'm going down and get something to eat and then start those carts rolling,' he concluded.

'Like the devil you will!' she blazed. 'You're dead on your feet. Don't forget, I own half the business and have something to say as to how it is run. You're going down and get something to eat, all right; and then you're going to come right back up here and go to bed.'

CHAPTER FOURTEEN

Under blue skies, through golden sunshine, the train rolled south the following morning.

The carters were in high spirits and shouted greetings and quips at Hatfield as he rode back and forth along the line to make sure all was in order. The outfit was working like a well oiled machine and Hatfield was pleased with its smooth efficiency.

Old Perkins was still excited and garrulous about Hatfield's tilt with the outlaws.

'Somehow I figured right from the start you'd come through whatever you were mixed up in,' he declared. 'The station manager wanted to send for the sheriff first off when we found your hat, but I couldn't see any sense in hauling the sheriff right back from Aguilar. What could he do? I talked him out of it.'

'The sheriff didn't stay in town overnight, then?'

'Nope,' replied Perkins. 'He left right after talking to Miss Pat. Kane Fisher had tied onto one of his wagons and they packed the stage guard's body back with them—he lived in Aguilar—and aimed to pick up what was left of Fisher's hands there under the cliff.'

'Fisher rode back with the sheriff?'

'That's right. He 'peared all worked up and bothered about something. Wanted to get back to Aguilar in a hurry.'

Hatfield nodded thoughtfully. He felt he had plenty to think about. It was fairly obvious that Kane Fisher was not the mysterious Boss the outlaws talked about. Hatfield was thoroughly baffled.

119

'Now I'm right back where I started,' he muttered under his breath. 'Don't know who to suspect.'

In contrast to the cheerfulness of the others, Pat Gomez was moody and depressed.

'I can't stop thinking of what those awful men might have done to you,' she explained. 'It's only by the mercy of God that you're alive today. I almost wish my father hadn't brought you here.'

'Is that so!'

'Stop it! you know what I mean,' she answered. 'Don't put things into my mouth I don't say. It's just that I'm worried sick over the danger you're constantly exposed to.'

'Could just as well have happened someplace else, under slightly different circumstances, and without the recompenses,' he said. 'It isn't every day that a man meets a girl like you.'

'You'd better not,' she warned. 'We Mexican women don't look kindly on too many rivals.'

'Who says you're Mexican?'

'Well, maybe I'm not,' she admitted, 'but my father is Spanish and my mother was a Texas girl of pure Irish extraction.'

'Good Lord!'

'Nice combination, isn't it?'

'About like mixing gunpowder and hot ashes,' he replied.

'Are you complaining?' she giggled.

'Nope, but I'm mindful of the explosive

120

potentials, of which I've had a sample.'

'Uh-huh, but who supplied the match?'

Hatfield gave up the argument; he felt he was coming out second best.

When they passed the shattered cliff the bodies of the unfortunate freighters had been removed and only the wrecked wagons and dead mules bore testimony to the tragedy. The rifled bales were still scattered around.

'Fisher didn't seem to pay 'em much mind,' commented Perkins. 'Said he'd send wagons to pick 'em up when he got around to it. Wonder how they got so busted? Those hellions must have planted a ton of dynamite under them rocks.'

'It was undoubtedly quite a blow,' Hatfield agreed.

The trip was made without incident and just at sunset the train rolled into Aguilar. Gomez was waiting at the station. He shook his head at his daughter in wordless disapproval but apparently thought scolding her was a waste of time.

'Don't ever get married, Hatfield,' he advised. 'See what you might be up against some day?'

'I don't think he'd mind so much,' Pat replied airily. 'Would you, Jim?'

'Perhaps not,' Hatfield admitted.

Gomez gave them a keen glace, stroked his mustache and did not comment.

After getting something to eat, Hatfield

returned to the station to check the rerouting of the loads, some of which would go to Presidio and across the Border, others to points east or west.

'The Old Man was sure worked up when word came of what happened to Fisher's wagons,' the station manager told Hatfield. 'Spent most of the day pacing the floor. And he didn't leave till Thomas got back from Sanders. Learning about that stage holdup didn't help matters much, I'm afraid. He spent the night in the rooming house. His room was next to mine and I heard him walking the floor again till all hours. Got me so nervous I couldn't sleep, either.'

'So he spent the night before last here in town?'

'That's right,' the manager nodded. 'Didn't go home. Said he wanted to be on hand if any more bad news came in.'

Hatfield sighed. He experienced a sense of relief that Gomez' movements were accounted for, but felt that things were getting more complicated by the minute.

Gomez and Pat dropped in a little later. 'We're going home,' the freighter said. 'Care to ride with us, Jim? I'd like to show you my place.'

'Not tonight,' Hatfield declined. 'I want to be on the job early to rearrange those Presidio loads. Too much space wasted in the packing; takes three carts for what two should be able

122

to handle. Maybe I can make it tomorrow night.'

Pat made a face at him behind her father's back, but Gomez nodded agreement.

'Just as you say,' he replied. 'The Presidio train won't roll for a couple of days. There is some stuff coming in from the west I want included. I'll see you tomorrow afternoon.'

They left the station, Pat making another face that seemed to say, 'just you wait!' Hatfield grinned at her and went back to work. Finally he shoved the papers aside and stood up.

'Think I'll go over to the Last Chance for a drink,' he announced. 'We've done enough for tonight.'

'Good notion,' agreed the manager. 'I'll go with you.'

At the Last Chance they found Perkins, Miguel and several others. After a couple of rounds of drinks, Perkins suggested a few hands of poker. They located a table and sat down. The dealer broke out a new deck of cards and spread them on the table. Hatfield started to pick one up, then stared at the back, his eyes narrowing. The intricate and rather unusual pattern was identical with that on the back of the marked deck he had taken off the slain rider on the Chihuahua Trail first time he had saved the ambushed cart train.

Hatfield played for about an hour, then, 'Think I'll go over to the bar and have a drink,' he told the others. 'My eyes are tired. I'll be back with you in a jiffy.'

Steve Ennis, the proprietor, was not in evidence. A jovial and talkative bartender with a handlebar mustache and an imposing spit curl plastered down over his forehead presided at the 'mahogany.' As he sipped his drink, Hatfield adroitly engaged him in conversation. After some inconsequential talk he remarked, 'I used to know a fellow who worked down this way, a dealer. A little thin-faced fellow with black hair and mole on his cheek. Wore glasses.'

The barkeep gave his spit curl a moment of careful consideration, before replying.

'Sounds like Joe Dawson who worked here for a while,' he said. 'Yep, it must have been Joe. Was a friend of Ennis, I think; they were always gabbin' together. Uh-huh, a scrawny little jigger but plenty salty even if he was a runt. Mighty handy with a sleeve gun. Handy with the pasteboards, too. He left about a month back. Don't know where he went. I figure him and Ennis knew each other before he worked here.'

'Those dealers are always on the move,' Hatfield commented. 'Wouldn't be surprised if he took a long trip.'

He deftly changed the subject and after another drink went back to the poker game.

Later, in his room, Hatfield compared the marked deck with a card he had deftly palmed during the game. He was not mistaken, the markings were identical.

'Now what's the tie-up here?' he mused. 'I played a long shot when I questioned that barkeep, and it paid off. That jigger worked for Ennis before he joined the raiding bunch, presumably handled by Kane Fisher. Or was he already tied up with the outfit? The Last Chance would be a good place to pick up bits of information. And he could have been planted in Fisher's outfit, that's another angle to consider. That raid on Fisher's cargo of silver dollars makes it look like somebody had the lowdown on what he does. That dealer apparently knew Ennis, which is probably how he got his job in the Last Chance. Quite a jigsaw puzzle and I've a notion that if I can fit the pieces together I'll have made considerable progress.'

He considered sounding out Ennis a bit but after some reflection decided against it.

One point was not to be overlooked. The removal of the two bodies before the sheriff arrived on the scene more than hinted that somebody feared one or both might be recognized if they were brought to town.

The following evening Hatfield rode to the Clover Leaf spread with Gomez. It was a good holding, he quickly concluded. A fine old ranchhouse built in the Spanish style, tight barns and other outbuildings in excellent repair. The land was first class range and what cattle he saw were in prime condition.

'I've a notion that even without the carting business you should be able to make out, sir,' he commented.

'Yes,' agreed Gomez. 'If it wasn't for the fact that continuing the freighting is a matter of pride with me, because it was begun by my grandfather and carried on by my father, I'd be inclined to give it up and live in peace and comfort on the proceeds of my ranch. My wants are simple and I have no one dependent on me but my daughter. In fact I suggested as much to her, but she couldn't see it at all. She says she doesn't intend to be run out of business by any such maverick as Kane Fisher, and as she said she mentioned to you, she does own half of it—my father left it to her—and she's of age. So you see,' he concluded with his wry smile, 'I couldn't quit if I wanted to.'

Hatfield enjoyed a good dinner and a pleasant evening with his host and his daughter. Gomez was an educated man and an entertaining conversationalist. Finally, however, he rose to his feet and smiled down at his guest.

'You young people can stay up as long as you want to, but I'm going to bed,' he said. 'An old man has to get his rest. Your room is at the head of the stairs, first on the right, Jim. I sleep in the rear of the house—last door down the hall. If you should want something during the night, don't hesitate to call me.'

126

'My room's right across the hall,' Pat remarked innocently. 'If you can't rouse Dad, call me. He sleeps like a log and snores something awful. I suppose all men snore.'

'I don't think I do,' Hatfield smiled.

As soon as she heard her father's door close, Pat drew a sheet of paper from a table drawer.

'Here's the list of the directors of the Clayton Mine,' she announced.

Hatfield took the list and studied the names. They included Gomez, Steve Ennis, and several names that meant nothing to him. Pat watched him curiously.

'Jim,' she said, when he looked up, 'can you tell me why you want those names?'

'Yes, I'll tell you,' Hatfield replied. 'That gold shipment of the stage was supposed to be a closely guarded secret, a scheme to foil a possible hold-up. It didn't work. Without a doubt, somebody talked, and to the wrong pair of ears. I figured it's logical that the directors would have known about the plan, and the mine manager, and quite likely nobody else but the guard and the stage driver. It's pretty certain that the guard and the driver didn't talk, but somebody did. The big question is, was it just a blabber-mouth, or was it done on purpose. That's why I'd like to learn something of the background of all concerned. What do you know about the manager?'

'He owns an interest in the mine and is, so

127

far as anybody knows, of irreproachable character.'

'And how about Jorgenson, first name on the list?'

'He owns the Swinging J, the best spread in the section.'

'And Pryor?'

'He is the proprietor of the town's largest general store and a vice-president of the bank.'

'How about Ridley?'

'He's president of the bank.'

'And Worthington?'

'That's Judge Worthington of the county court.'

Hatfield shook his head and sighed. 'Hardly the sort that would be given to loose talking or a tie-up with owlhoots,' he observed morosely.

'And it leaves only Dad and Steve Ennis,' Pat pointed out.

'Uh-huh, only your dad and Steve Ennis,' Hatfield agreed. 'And your dad is a rich man or mighty close to it, and Ennis owns a prosperous saloon and a ranch. Right back where we started! Oh, the devil! I'm going to bed, too.'

CHAPTER FIFTEEN

On the morning of the second day, the Presidio train got under way. Hatfield knew it was a fifty-mile trip, a good part of it over the burning desert, and couldn't be made in a single day. Aside from the natural difficulties to be overcome, he did not anticipate any trouble. He felt that Kane Fisher was not likely to meddle with the Gomez trains for a while, at least. Perkins felt the same way.

'What happened under that cliff up toward Sanders must have given Kane a mite to think about,' he observed shrewdly. 'He knew for sure none of our boys had anything to do with that and must have put in a lot of time wondering who did, unless he's into a row with somebody we don't know about. Wonder if that could be it? I'll have to admit the thing's got me a bit puzzled. Why should anybody drygulch a shipment of hides and wool?'

'As I said before, there might have been other goods of value,' Hatfield replied.

'Maybe,' Perkins admitted, 'but if there wasn't five wagonloads of stuff laying around there I miss my guess. If there was something else it must have been mighty small in bulk. Fisher don't freight no gold or anything like that.'

Hatfield nodded and did not comment.

'That rukus did us some good in another way,' Perkins continued. 'Gomez don't drygulch no trains, but don't you think for a minute some of our Mexican boys wouldn't, as a sort of get-even chore. Those folks are long on blood feuds. They're a peaceful lot but they've been mighty fed up with what's been going on of late. What happened that night just north of Aguilar was mighty nigh to the last straw. There was some talk going on. But Fisher's wagons getting blown to the devil puzzled them and gave them something else to think about and tempers time to cool. I don't figure we'll have any trouble with them unless something else busts loose.'

Hatfield was inclined to think Perkins might have the right of it. He also was familiar with the mercurial Mexican temperament.

The trip was made without incident and late in the afternoon of the second day out found the carts safe in the old town of sun-baked adobe houses, a minor port of entry with the Mexican pueblo of Ojinaga directly across the Rio Grande, squatting like an aged hombre in the shade of giant cottonwoods.

In Presidio as in Sanders, Hatfield met with complaints. ⇌

'This is the first Gomez train to come in on schedule in weeks,' one storekeeper declared.

'You can depend on them arriving when promised from now on,' Hatfield assured him.

'I hope so,' the other replied. 'Suppose you've got stuff for Ojinaga across the River?'

'Quite a few loads,' Hatfield admitted.

'Reckon you'll get a scolding over there, too. They've been having their troubles, what with delays of shipments from up north and Javelina and his hellions swallerforkin' around and knocking off valuable shipments. He's given this section a rest for the past couple of weeks, though. Cooking up some extra hellishness, I suppose. Well, good luck!'

Hatfield had no trouble clearing with the Customs officials. The carts were given but a perfunctory inspection.

'We don't worry about Gomez,' the inspector said. 'Never have had any trouble with him. Okay, shove 'em across.'

Hatfield did find the Ojinaga traders disgruntled, but, speaking fluent Spanish, he soon won their confidence.

'We like to deal with *Don* Sebastion,' they declared, 'but we must have our shipments when promised. Goods pile up here while waiting for him to take them. *Gracias, Captain*, we hope that things will be better in the future.'

Hatfield hoped so, too. They would have to be if Gomez was to stay in the carting business.

'Well, what do you think of the situation?' Perkins asked as the heavily laden carts rolled northward two days later.

'Here's how the situation stands,' Hatfield replied. 'Goods must be delivered and picked up when promised. Those fellows are up against increasing competition. The country's filling up, railroads are building, Eastern aggregations of captial are beginning to get interested in this section. First thing we know we may have real competition. The old easy-

131

going methods are doomed. I'm going to have a serious talk with Gomez and see if I can't get him to shift to big wagons and a rigid schedule that must be fulfilled at all costs.'

'Better have the talk with Miss Pat,' Perkins suggested shrewdly. 'I got a notion she's taking over and it won't be long before she has the whole say as to what is to be done. I think the Old Man is slipping a bit. Strain's too much for him.'

Hatfield nodded. He was developing something of a similar notion.

They were about twenty miles south of Aguilar on the second day out when, on topping a rise, Perkins shaded his eyes with his hand and peered ahead.

'Looks like one of Kane Fisher's trains headed this way,' he remarked. 'Six big wagons and making good time. Reckon that's Kane riding out in front. Now all we need is for somebody to do or say the wrong thing and there'll be fireworks.'

Hatfield did not think that Fisher would make any hostile move against the big train, but with the hazards of short tempers and resentments in mind, he alerted the guards and drivers.

'I don't want you fellows starting any trouble,' he told them. 'But if somebody else starts it, I expect you to take care of anything that busts loose. On your toes, now!'

He rode back to the head of the train,

where Perkins was pacing his horse a hundred yards or so in front of the foremost cart.

'Jim!' he exclaimed excitedly, as Hatfield rode up, 'I don't think that's Fisher riding out in front. Ain't wide enough for him. Say! I believe it's that store-keepin' feller at Sanders, Clem Haskins.'

'It is,' Hatfield agreed. 'Now what the devil!'

He quickened the pace of his horse and a little later drew rein beside Haskins. The storekeeper eyed him with what Hatfield interpreted as an expression of malicious satisfaction on his sardonic face.

'Howdy,' he said. 'Told you I figured I might do something about them delays. I did it. I've started my own freighting business.'

'Not a bad notion,' Hatfield replied. 'Maybe there's enough business in this section to keep three outfits going.'

'There'd better be,' Haskins said, adding significantly, ' 'cause I aim to get my share.'

With a twisted grin he rode on. Hatfield gazed after him a moment.

'Now what's that jigger got up his sleeve?' he wondered. 'He knows darn well there isn't enough business for three outfits.'

'Reckon he figures to take business away from Gomez and Fisher,' Perkins said, 'and I've a notion he'll do it if we don't step lively.'

Hatfield was gazing at the approaching wagons. They were excellent vehicles, brand-new, spacious. The mules that drew them were sturdy and in fine condition. The loads were neatly covered with tarpaulins drawn down snug.

Perkins was paying more attention to the drivers and guards.

'Whe-e-ew!' he muttered. 'Did you ever see a saltier looking lot! Haskins must have busted open a calaboose and turned loose all the prize specimens!'

Hatfield was inclined to agree that the specimens in question were hard looking characters. They nodded in a noncommittal fashion, however, as the wagons rolled past and some of them voiced gruff greetings. Hatfield felt that their attitude was strictly impersonal. They seemed not at all affected by the suspicious glances cast in their direction by the Gomez guards and drivers as they passed the cart train.

Perkins was shaking his head and scratching his scraggly whiskers. 'Well, what do you think about it?' he asked.

'I don't know yet,' Hatfield replied.

'Wonder why that jigger all of a sudden took a notion to horn it?'

'I don't think it was an all-of-a-sudden notion,' Hatfield said. 'Takes time to get together an outfit like that and make business connections. I'd say he'd been planning it for quite a while.'

Perkins looked thoughtful. 'A while back, the way things were going, I reckon it did look like a chance for another outfit to come in and skim off the cream,' he observed. 'Sort of different since you took charge.'

'Maybe,' Hatfield conceded, 'but once he'd started he couldn't very well pull back. Well, it's up to us to give him a run for his money, that's all.'

'Wonder how Kane Fisher will take it?'

'That's something that warrants serious consideration,' Hatfield replied. 'Fisher seems good at going off half-cocked and I've a notion he won't take at all kindly to it.'

'Fisher's got a salty outfit, but I figure that bunch can give him as good as he sends,' said Perkins. 'Okay, let 'em fight! Just so they leave us alone.'

As foreman of Sebastian Gomez' carting trains, Hatfield was inclined to agree, but as a Texas Ranger, sworn to uphold law and order, he did not look on the prospect with favor. One of his chores in the section was to prevent a bloody cart war such as they had at Goliad. Haskins' entry into the picture certainly did not improve the situation.

But there was another angle to which Hatfield was giving serious thought. In his mind was growing a vague and nebulous idea that related to Haskins' decision to engage in the carting business. A rather far-fetched notion, he was forced to admit, but the Lone Wolf was given to playing hunches, and right now he had a hunch. He proceeded to put it into practice after the train arrived at Aguilar and the various chores connected with the completion of the trip were taken care of. He summoned Miguel Allende, the captain of the Mexican guards.

'Miguel,' he told the young Mexican, 'I've got a job for you. I want you to ride to Ojinaga and find out if Haskins delivered his goods there rather than at Presidio. Learn, if you can, who received them and if Haskins picked up stuff for the trip north at the same place or places. Find out all you can about those places, how long they've been in business, who runs them, and so on. Think you can do it?'

'*Si, Capitan*, I will learn all,' Miguel promised. Hatfield was confident he would be as good as his word.

After two days of preparation, the northbound train for Sanders got under way. Pat wanted to go along, but this time Hatfield was firm.

'Not until things quiet down,' he told her. 'Besides, you're too darn distracting. I can't keep my mind on my business. I promise I'll drop over to the house as soon as we get back.'

'You'd better!' she declared. 'And you'll be careful, won't you. Jim?'

'Of course; I always am.'

Pat looked far from convinced.

CHAPTER SIXTEEN

After the train left Aguilar, Hatfield was more than usually alert. He had a feeling something was going to happen. He had had that feeling before and had learned not to dismiss it lightly. His keen eyes probed every thicket and grove and he gave much attention to the long slopes that so often overlooked the trail. They were usually thickly wooded and would give shelter to most anything. The movements of birds came in for careful scrutiny, for he had long ago learned that they would often give warning of something unfamiliar on the ground beneath where they were perched.

A little after noon the trail was winding along the base of a long slope that terminated in an almost unbroken line of cliffs less than a fifth of a mile higher up. The slope was covered with thick brush, but Hatfield suspected that along the base of the cliffs was comparatively clear ground. He gave the shadowy slope the most careful attention.

Suddenly his every sense was at hair-trigger alertness. From far up the slope had come a sound—a drumming whir that he knew was made by the wings of a covey of grouse abruptly taking the air.

'Now what set those speckled bellies off?' he wondered. 'Grouse usually don't cut loose like that in brush. They run a ways and then take wing one at a time. Only when something startles them do they sift sand all together that way. Of course, it could be only a prowling coyote or a weasel, but not likely at this time of the day.'

He studied the approximate spot from which the sound had come but could see nothing. The grouse did not take off again.

'Just the same, I've a notion it will stand a mite of investigation, coupled with other things I've been noticing.'

He turned and called to Perkins, who was riding a little ways back along the train.

'I've a feeling somebody is pacing us up there on the sag,' he told the guard captain when he drew alongside. 'Several times I've seen birds rise up suddenly for no apparent good reason. And that bunch of grouse that just cut loose acted like something was coming up on them. Maybe nothing to it, but I think I'll have a little look.'

'Think somebody is waiting for a chance to take a shot at one of us?' Perkins asked nervously.

'Could be,' Hatfield admitted. 'I figure he's up along the base of the cliffs, if he's there at all. Too far for anything like accurate shooting at a downward angle, but farther on there might be someplace where he'd get a better chance. See that bulge in the trail about half a mile ahead? If I can get around that bulge in a hurry, I'll be out of his sight for a while. Then I'll slide up the slope and be quite a bit ahead of him. I'll hole up and wait, and if there is somebody up there, maybe I can get a look at him.'

'Damn risky business, I'd say,' replied Perkins. 'Suppose he sees you first?'

'I'll risk it,' Hatfield said. 'Keep the train moving just as it is. Don't speed up, and don't hang back. Be seeing you. Trail! Goldy!'

Instantly the great sorrel shot forward at a dead run. Perkins watched Hatfield's diminishing figure and swore under his breath. He saw horse and man vanish around the bend.

'Now I got the jumps,' he complained, 'and I will have till he shows up again. Maybe there really ain't nobody up there. Feller gets notions when he's sort of expecting something to happen.'

After rounding the bulge, Hatfield gave Goldy free rein for another half mile. Then he pulled him to a halt. He scanned the slope for a moment and turned the sorrel into the brush and sent him steadily upward for about half the distance to the cliffs. In a dense thicket he pulled him to a halt and dismounted.

'Stay put, and don't sing any songs,' he warned. He continued up the slope on foot, taking advantage of all cover, careful to break no twig, to dislodge no stone. A little distance below the cliffs he paused. As he suspected, a belt of almost bare ground flanked the cliff base, and along it ran what he decided was once an old Indian trail, doubtless used by aborigines who had designs on anything passing along the Chihuahua below.

Close to the track, Hatfield took shelter behind a clump of growth. 'Now if there really is somebody up here and he comes ambling along as I figure he will any minute, he won't be in shape to do any arguing back when I suggest a mite of a talk is in order,' he told himself.

Slowly the minutes passed, and no sound of approaching hoof beats broke the silence. Nothing moved in the open space beyond where Hatfield crouched. It began to look as if he had only imagined there was somebody riding the head of the slope, or his quarry had turned back. Then abruptly his nerves tensed like tautly drawn wire.

From a little distance to the north of where he crouched had sounded a faint snap, as if a careful walker had inadvertently trodden on a rotten stick under the fallen leaves. He strained his ears, but the sound was not repeated. The silence remained unbroken as before. Cautiously he groped about and found a fragment of stone. With a swift underhand motion he tossed it down the slope and a little to the front. It crackled through a clump of brush, affording a creditable imitation of somebody falling over a log.

The result was instant and startling. From where he had heard the slight sound burst a roar of gunfire. Twigs and leaves leaped into the air as bullets raked the clump of brush from side to side.

Hatfield jerked his own guns. Before the echoes had slammed back from the cliff face, both muzzles were spouting flame and smoke. He in turn raked the growth with a rain of lead.

There was a startled curse, a yelp of pain. Then a prodigious crashing as somebody went away from there in a hurry. Hatfield leaped forward and found himself entangled in a mat of mesquite thorns. Before he could win clear of the tenacious growth, the crashing in the brush was replaced by a drumming of hoofs that quickly faded into the distance.

With a few well chosen curses, Hatfield ejected the spent shells from his guns and replaced them with fresh cartridges. Then he holstered his Colts and headed back to where he had left Goldy.

'A smooth gent,' he told Goldy. 'Yep, a jigger with plenty of savvy. He figured out just what I was up to when I speeded up down there on the trail. He speeded up, too, and he had a short cut across the bulge. Holed up waiting for me to ride along that track when he didn't show up. As I would have done if it hadn't been for him stepping on that dead branch and giving himself away. Otherwise the first I'd have known of his being around would have been when I leaned against the hot end of a slug. Uh-huh, salty, and with brains. Horse, we're up against a smart outfit, and they're out to get us. This time we got the breaks, even though we were outsmarted. Better not slip again, though. Can't depend on the luck holding. I nicked that jigger, anyhow, judging from the way he yelped, though evidently not enough to do him much damage. I don't think we need to worry about him anymore today, but we still don't know for sure just why he was up here. Maybe we can find out. We'll follow that hog track for a spell and see if anything interesting shows.'

He rode north along the shadowy thread of trail that hugged the base of the cliffs. A mile farther on the cliffs began to edge downward until they ran only a couple of hundred yards from the base of the slope. Below, they were reproduced by a similar escarpment about twenty feet high, beyond which was the open rangeland. Toward the lower cliffs the trail gradually edged until it ran no great distance from their crest.

Another third of a mile and the trail dipped into a little hollow and continued only a few yards from the lip of the cliffs. Hatfield pulled Goldy to a halt and gazed downward. Not fifty yards distant, to be seen through the straggle of growth, was the Chihuahua Trail. He gave a low whistle. 'Blazes! What a setup!' he muttered. 'Fifty men could hole up here, and anything down there on the trail would be at their mercy. No chance to ride up and root them out, and the bank would give them cover. Maybe this is why that hellion was prowling around here, getting the lowdown. Horse, when we head back from Sanders I'm going to play a hunch!'

He rode on. The lower cliffs continued for perhaps a quarter of a mile farther before they were replaced by a gentle slope. Hatfield rode down to the trail and pulled up. He knew he must be some distance ahead of the slow-moving train. He hooked one leg comfortably over the saddle horn, rolled a cigarette and waited.

After a while he heard the grinding of tires on the stones and the train came into view around a bend. Old Si Perkins, riding in front, gave a shout of relief and quickened his horse's pace.

'We heard the shooting and didn't know what the hell had busted loose, but we obeyed orders and didn't come looking for you,' he said as soon as he was within talking distance.

'Glad you didn't,' Hatfield replied. 'There was somebody up there, all right, but he outsmarted me and gave me the slip.'

Perkins cast an apprehensive glace at the slope. 'Every time I look there I get a funny feeling between my shoulder blades,' he growled.

'Don't think we have anything more to worry about today,' Hatfield reassured him. 'The jigger sure hightailed and I've a notion he kept on going. And we'll be in the hills in another hour.'

It was almost sundown when they sighted Sanders. To their astonishment, the level ground just south of the town was a scene of bustling activity. Graders and steam shovels and a corps of pick and shovel men were busily at work. A surveyor was taking sights with a transit.

Motioning the train to proceed, Hatfield and Perkins pulled up alongside the surveyor.

'What's going on?' the Ranger asked.

The surveyor, a pleasant faced young man, smiled up at Hatfield.

'Howdy, cowboy,' he replied. 'We're building a railroad.'

'You mean the C. & P. is coming through here?' Hatfield asked in surprise. 'I understood they figured to go through north of Sanders Canyon.'

'Reckon that's what most folks thought,' the surveyor chuckled. 'The change of plans was pretty much a secret. If it had been known in advance that the road was coming through here, the price of land would have shot up sky-high. Old Jaggers Dunn, the General Manager, operated through an agent and bought up all the land we'll need at a reasonable price. Going to build shops and

144

roundhouse and big yards here.'

As they rode on, Perkins slapped his thigh with a horny hand. 'Now I see why Clem Haskins got into the freighting business,' he chuckled. 'He must have found out the road was coming through here. This town is going to boom.'

Hatfield nodded but did not comment. He agreed that Sanders was due to boom, but he doubted if the coming of the railroad would greatly affect the carting business one way or another. It might cut down on the east and west trade a bit; but unless the railroad decided to run a line down to Presidio, which it might eventually do, freighting by cart and wagon from the south would continue about the same as before.

Haskins, however, might think otherwise. And if he had been influenced by an advance knowledge of the coming of the railroad, a theory Hatfield had been carefully building up was all of a sudden knocked to pieces.

'Seems I'm always getting started, and then getting right back where I started,' he mused morosely.

After transacting necessary business matters with the station manager, Hatfield repaired to the Cattleman's Hotel restaurant for something to eat. As he entered, he spotted a familiar face. Seated at a nearby table was Steve Ennis.

The Last Chance owner waved a greeting.

'Come over and take a load off your feet,' he invited.

Hatfield sat down opposite Ennis, who regarded him with his pale eyes.

'Get your carts through okay?' he asked.

'No trouble,' Hatfield replied. 'What brings you up into this neck of the woods?'

Ennis smiled with his lips; Hatfield had noted before that a smile never seemed to reach his eyes.

'Looking things over,' he replied. 'Guess you heard about the railroad coming through here? Well, I got a tip to that effect a few days ago. Decided it might not be a bad notion to open up a place here if I can tie onto a good site; I figure this town is going to boom.'

'Wouldn't be surprised,' Hatfield admitted. 'The surveyor down on the grade told me they intend to put in shops and yards, and railroaders are always good drinkers, at least that's been my experience.'

'Mine, too,' said Ennis. He moved in his chair and his lips abruptly compressed as if from pain.

'Here comes a waiter for your order,' he said. 'Have this one on me. Your outfit brings plenty of business into my place.'

Ennis finished eating first. 'Well, I'm going out and look around a bit,' he said. 'Want to head back to Aguilar first thing in the morning. Be seeing you.'

He stood up, winced, gripped the table top

146

as if for support.

'Damn it!' he exclaimed. 'My horse pitched me the other day and I think maybe I strained a tendon. Hurts like hell every now and then.'

'It can cause plenty of trouble, and for a long time,' Hatfield agreed as he instinctively glanced down.

For an instant his gaze fixed on the top of Ennis' fancily stitched riding boot, then drifted away. Ennis grinned wryly and walked out with a decided limp.

Hatfield sat staring after him, the concentration furrow deep between his black brows, a sure sign the Lone Wolf was doing some hard thinking. In that swift glance he had noted that the top of Steve Ennis' riding boot was shredded and torn, and just above the tear, the dark cloth of his riding breeches was stained darker by what was undoubtedly fresh blood.

Hatfield rolled and lighted a cigarette, and remarked to the glowing tip, 'The Immortal Bard of Avon, as old Tom Conley would put it, once said, "Thus conscience does make cowards of us all." He might have added that conscience also makes folks lie when the truth, or something close to it, would serve them a lot better. Senor Ennis was nicked in the leg by a bullet only a few hours back! Things are beginning to tie up; but I'm still a hell of a long ways from being in a position to drop my loop!'

CHAPTER SEVENTEEN

The night before starting back to Aguilar, Hatfield called his guards together in the station office and told them of what he discovered on the slope above the Chihuahua Trail.

'That place is a natural for a drygulching,' he explained. 'A bunch holed up there could kill every man with the train, and with very little risk to themselves, and I'm of the opinion that the outfit we're up against is capable of doing just that.'

His audience stared at him in consternation. 'What the blazes are we going to do about it?' asked Perkins.

'I figure to play a hunch,' Hatfield replied. 'If we can sneak up on them while they're waiting for the train to show, we can get the upper hand. Maybe they'll be there, maybe they won't. Perhaps me throwing lead at that jigger will have scared them off, but I'm working on the supposition that I didn't. I believe they'll be there. I won't deny that we'll be taking one big chance. Let something go wrong and we'll very likely get blown from under our hats. So if anybody doesn't feel quite up to the chore, say so now.'

Felipe, Miguel Allende's assistant, shrugged his broad shoulders and voiced the concensus of opinion.

'*Capitan,*' he said, 'where you lead we will follow.'

'Okay,' Hatfield nodded. 'Felipe, you pick the two best shots of your bunch, and Perkins, the best two of yours. That'll be enough. The others stick with the train.'

'Don't think you others are being slighted,' he added with a grim smile, 'if we slip up somehow, you gents will be the setting quail. Now I guess I don't need to tell you to keep a tight latigo on your jaws. If what we plan to do should happen to reach the wrong ears, well, we won't have any use for ears after tomorrow.'

The following morning the train rolled south under an overcast sky. The whole vast sweep of the heavens was a leaden arch that seemed to press down on the cowering earth. The air was heavy and dank and there was no wind. The mules, sensitive to weather conditions, plodded dully with hanging heads and drooping ears. The horses, on the contrary, were jumpy and ill at ease. It was a depressing day and not calculated to improve nerves already taut to the breaking point.

'There's one thing in our favor, though,' Hatfield said as he eyed the clouds of mist swathing the upper slopes in an opaque veil. 'There won't be anybody up at the top of the sag keeping a lookout. They can't spot us from a distance.'

At the apex of a bend a little to the north of where he reached the trail on the day of his encounter with the watcher on the slope, Hatfield called his men together.

'Here's where we go,' he told them. 'We'll follow that old track up there for a little less than a quarter of a mile, then we'll tie the horses and slip along on foot.'

He had already instructed the drivers to keep the carts moving steadily but slowly.

'And keep your eyes peeled and be ready for anything if we happen to slip up,' he cautioned them. 'Let's go,' he told his men.

They negotiated the first leg of the expedition without incident, leaving the horses tethered in a thicket and stealing forward cautiously for some distance. Finally Hatfield held up his hand.

'Now comes a ticklish part,' he whispered. 'We've got to slide up into the brush and work around till we get in behind them, if they're there. The important thing is no noise. Fortunately sounds won't travel well in this heavy air, but don't take any chances.'

Silently as ghosts they entered the brush, climbed the slope for a little ways and then turned parallel to the track.

It was nerve wracking work. Every slight sound was magnified by imagination. Their breathing seemed to be loud pants, the beating of their hearts a low thunder. Twigs touched by a passing sleeve let out shrill shrieks of protest. The almost inaudible whisper of boot soles on soft ground was an appalling crunching. When somebody kicked a bunch of dry leaves they rustled like a nest of aroused snakes and Hatfield felt his hatband grow moist against his forehead. The less than a hundred yards they had to cover stretched out into endless miles.

With the plainsman's acute sense of distance and direction, Hatfield knew when they must be about opposite the little hollow where the old trail dipped below the cliff lip. He turned the course downward and they crept forward at a pace that any able-bodied snail would have left standing still. Behind a final fringe of twigs and leaves they halted, peering into the shadowy hollow, and saw dim shapes crouched there. Hatfield counted seven altogether. Anyhow, the odds were even.

Hatfield hesitated. The sensible thing would be to cut loose without warning. Those cold killers were utterly devoid of mercy and deserved none themselves. They were waiting to ruthlessly murder men who had never done them any harm.

But the code of the Rangers said no! A peace officer must announce himself and his intentions. And that code was solidly built on the unalterable principles of human rights and orderly justice. He started to open his lips, and the unpredictable happened. A guard, nervously shifting his weight, trod on a loose stone that rolled beneath his foot. He reeled, floundered, and fell, his cocked gun going off with a crash like the crack of doom. The shapes below wheeled around, steel gleamed.

'Let 'em have it!' Hatfield roared. He jerked his guns and fired as fast as he could pull trigger. His companions already had theirs in their hands. Answering shots boomed from the hollow. Smoke swirled and eddied in impenetrable clouds, split by lances of reddish flame as the battlers blasted death at each other through the murk.

Above the roar of the guns, Hatfield heard a crashing of brush, then a crackling beat of hoofs. He abruptly realized that no more answering shots were coming from the hollow.

'Hold it!' he shouted. 'Hold it—all over!'

The shooting stopped, the smoke cloud slowly lifted, revealing stark shapes sprawled and huddled grotesquely on the ground below. Guns ready for instant action, Hatfield stole forward, the others following. After a quick glance around he holstered his Colts. There was no more danger from the four outlaws who remained in the hollow. They were thoroughly and satisfactorily dead.

'Three got away,' the Ranger muttered. 'We made a pretty good bag, though.'

He took stock of his own casualties. One guard was dead, shot squarely between the eyes. Another had a bullet through his shoulder, high up. Old Si Perkins was cursing venomously as he swabbed at a gashed cheek that Hatfield decided was of little consequence save for the scar that must remain, a scar that would not be particularly noticed among Si's already outstanding collection. He proceeded to bind up the punctured shoulder with strips torn from his shirt.

'That should hold you till we get to town,' he decided. 'It isn't bad—no bones broken. Here, drag on this cigarette, it should help.' He turned to the others.

'Some of you scout around and see if you can locate the horses these jiggers rode,' he ordered. 'Brands might tell us something. Felipe, you slide down the cliff—I think you can make it—and halt the carts when they get here.'

Hatfield examined the slain outlaws. They were hard looking specimens with nothing outstanding about any of them. Nobody could recall ever having seen them before. Their pockets revealed a miscellany of articles but nothing of any particular significance aside from considerable sums of money.

'Business has been good with them, all right,' Perkins commented. 'Think they might be part of the bunch that robbed the stage?'

'Quite likely,' Hatfield replied.

'And not part of Kane Fisher's outfit?'

'I don't think so,' the Ranger said. 'I've a notion Fisher is sort of lying low nowdays.'

'Javelina's bunch?'

'Could be,' Hatfield admitted.

The guards who were searching for the horses returned with four, saddled and bridled.

'They were tied in the brush right up the track,' one announced. 'And we saw blood spots on the leaves.'

'One of the three that got away was wounded, eh?' Hatfield commented.

'*Si, Capitan*, perhaps more.'

The horses were good stock and equipped with first class rigs. The brands, however, were meaningless skillet-of-snakes Mexican burns.

'We'll take them along,' Hatfield decided. 'Load the dead guard's body on one and the wounded man can ride. We'll leave those other jiggers where they are for the sheriff. Suppose he'll scold us for taking the law into our own hands again, but we really didn't have time to send for him. Okay, let's go!'

They started on the weary trudge back to where they left their horses and finally made it to the trail. Pushing ahead they soon overtook the carts that had halted under the ominous cliff. The wounded guard was made comfortable in one of the carts and the train proceeded.

'Think we'll have any more trouble?' Perkins asked.

'Not likely today,' Hatfield replied. 'Those sidewinders got a rough going over they didn't expect.'

'Wish we'd done for all of the buzzards,'

Perkins growled vindictively. 'Damn shame three of them had to get away.'

'Yes, and one of them was very likely somebody important,' Hatfield said. 'The quick thinkers are always the ones that slide out of a rukus like that.'

When the train arrived at Aguilar, Hatfield found Miguel Allende back from Ojinaga with his report on the movements of Clem Haskins.

'There's a new store in Ojinaga and to it Haskins has delivered his goods,' Miguel said. 'There, too, he picked up goods for the return trip. I loitered around the Customs House with my sombrero drawn low and my serape muffled about my face and heard the goods declared. Fine merchandise, all—articles of gold and silver, products of the looms of Mexico, unusual bead work, and other things of great worth. Goods that bring high prices in the East. He paid a heavy duty, but doubtless his profit will be high.'

'Plenty high, the chances are,' Hatfield agreed with a significance that Miguel did not catch. 'Any idea who owns that new store?'

'There is talk that an American owns it, but it has a Mexican manager,' Miguel replied.

'Wonder if Haskins himself might own it?'

'That is possible,' Miguel conceded, 'but as to the truth I cannot say.'

Hatfield dropped in at the Last Chance. 'Ennis around?' he asked the bartender.

'Nope,' that worthy replied. 'Said he was

155

going up to Sanders again yesterday. Supposed to be back today, but so far he hasn't showed up. Wasn't feeling so good; hurt his leg.'

'Hurt it last week, didn't he?' Hatfield asked.

'Dunno,' said the barkeep. 'He didn't mention it till day before yesterday when he came in limping.'

Accompanied by Perkins, Hatfield hunted up the sheriff and reported the attempted drygulching. The sheriff gave him an injured look.

'Ever since you landed here, all I do is ride around and collect bodies,' he complained querulously, 'What you trying to do—depopulate the county?'

'I wasn't responsible for those under the cliff below Sanders,' Hatfield pointed out.

'No, but you found them. You're a bad luck piece if there ever was one. Why don't you go back where you came from?'

'Maybe I will before long,' Hatfield predicted cheerfully.

'I hope so,' grunted the sheriff. 'I'm beginning to feel like an undertaker. Wish I was one. Undertakers hereabouts get rich. Yes, I'll ride up there tomorrow. And hold up your next killing for a day or two, won't you? So I can get a night's sleep.'

Chuckling over the sheriff's indignation, Hatfield and Perkins went back to the Last Chance. They were there when Steve Ennis came in, around midnight. His clothes were powdered with dust, his face was haggard and he looked in anything but a good temper. Also he limped badly. He spotted Hatfield and Perkins, nodded shortly and disappeared through a door that led to the back room. Fifteen minutes later he reappeared, the dust removed and looking somewhat refreshed. After talking with several patrons at the bar, he strolled over to Hatfield's table and eased himself into a vacant chair.

'Leg's still bothering me,' he announced, wincing a little as he changed his position. 'I saw your train pull out of Sanders this morning. I was in Clem Haskins' store. Spent most of the day dickering with him for that vacant lot next to the store. That's where I figure to build my new place. He's a shrewd number and a hard man to deal with. I've a notion he'll give Gomez and Fisher a run for their money in the carting business. I wouldn't want him for a competitor.'

'Competition keeps folks on their toes,' Hatfield observed.

'That's right,' agreed Ennis, 'but just the same I hope he doesn't take a notion to get into the saloon business. Have a good trip?'

'Fair to middling,' Hatfield replied. 'It was a heavy day.'

'Blamed heavy. Air seemed to press down like a blanket. Thought all the time it was going to rain, but it never did. Well, I'm going to check the day's take and then go to bed. I'll send over a drink.'

With a nod he got to his feet, rather painfully, and went to the bar.

'A nice feller,' commented Perkins as he sipped the drink on the house. 'Always does the right thing.'

'Perhaps not always,' Hatfield remarked with a slight smile.

Hatfield rode to the Clover Leaf ranch house and had a serious talk with Gomez. He told him of the coming of the railroad to Sanders and of Clem Haskins' getting into the freighting business.

'So you see, sir, you're all of a sudden up against serieus competition,' he concluded, 'I'm afraid you'll have to do something about it.'

Gomez stroked his mustache and looked grave. 'What would you suggest?' he asked.

'First off,' Hatfield replied, 'I'd replace the old carts with modern wagons and equipment. Then I'd negotiate a contract with the railroad to haul stuff they'll bring in for the mines and ranches and towns over to the southwest. There'll be a big demand for a lot of things now that freight can reach Sanders by rail.'

Pat answered for her father. 'We'll do it, Jim,' she declared. 'I've been trying to talk Dad into modernizing the business for quite a while. Now maybe he'll listen.'

'I can get wagons quickly from San

Antonio,' Gomez said, 'but I don't know how to go about getting a contract with the railroad.'

'I think I can lend you a hand there,' Hatfield offered. 'I happen to know an official of the road.'

He did not mention that the official was none other than General Manager James G. 'Jaggers' Dunn, his close personal friend.

'All right,' Gomez replied, smiling his wry smile. 'They say you can't teach an old dog new tricks, but I guess it largely depends on the teacher. Jim, do you always get everything you go after?'

'Oh, not always,' Hatfield returned lightly, with a glance at Pat. 'Sometimes it's brought to me.'

The answering look he got was one of those that says, 'Just you wait till I get you alone!'

The next morning Gomez put in an order for fifty of the biggest and best freighting wagons obtainable. Hatfield wrote a letter to General Manager Dunn.

CHAPTER EIGHTEEN

Three nights later, an acrimonious discussion raged in the back room of Clem Haskins' store. Haskins was there, half a dozen hard looking characters, and Steve Ennis.

159

'I tell you if that big Texas buzzard is allowed to run around loose much longer he's going to catch onto something sure as blazes!' Haskins declared.

'He seems to bear a charmed life,' Ennis said. 'I'm still trying to figure how he got out of that cabin alive. Barnes swears that when he left to come for me he was unarmed, half dead from a crack on the head, and with Butch holding a gun on him. Just the same he managed to kill Butch and Slim and walk out. And the other day when I was trailing that cart train he spotted me up on the slope, though I know darned well I kept under cover all the time. When he speeded up that infernal yellow horse I knew he had spotted me. So I rode ahead and laid for him. And what happened! He outsmarted me and drilled a hole through the calf of my leg. And how in hell did he catch on to what we had planned for the train? It was just luck that I got out of that rukus with nothing worse than another hunk of meat knocked loose. He's plumb poison if anybody ever was!'

'You've got a reputation for being sort of poison yourself, Steve,' Haskins observed dryly. 'If he can't be handled by—'

'Never mind that!' Ennis snapped.

'—by you, who in hell can handle him?'

'I don't know, but it's got to be done, and without delay,' Ennis returned. 'I do know that he's killed six of our best men and somehow managed to throw a scare into Kane Fisher that's caused him to lay off the Gomez trains, and just when we thought we had it arranged nicely for them to beat each other's brains out.'

'Do you think he might suspect you're—' Haskins began.

'I said never mind that!' Ennis interrupted angrily. 'Why should he suspect me of anything? He's more apt to suspect you. You look the part.'

Haskins chuckled, as if he found whatever Ennis meant amusing.

'What we need is a rip-snorting cart war between Gomez and Fisher,' Ennis resumed. 'One with plenty of killings. Then the Rangers would move in and put both outfits out of business. They did just that after the big fight over at Goliad. They went to court and got an order restraining both companies from operating, on the grounds that they were a menace to law and order. They're still fighting it in the courts, trying to get the injunction lifted, and meanwhile other outfits have taken over their business. That could easily happen here. Fisher's hands aren't clean, and quite a few people think Gomez is Javelina. The Rangers wouldn't have any trouble getting an injunction.'

'Rangers is bad business,' one of the gathering remarked nervously. 'I don't hanker to have them around.'

'We'd have nothing to worry about from them,' Ennis insisted. 'Attention would be concentrated on Gomez and Fisher. We'd just take over the legitimate freighting business and lay low for a while. That would be a good notion in more ways than one. If everything was quiet hereabouts for a spell, folks would begin to believe that Gomez really was Javelina and that the Rangers had scared him into taking cover. Then later we'd start operating again, with fatter pickings than ever. The big problem is how to start trouble between those two outfits again. I'm beginning to get an idea how it might be worked.'

'I figure the big problem right now is how to get rid of that sidewinder Hatfield,' said Haskins. 'Everything was going along nicely till he showed up.'

'And I'm beginning to get an idea how that can be done, too,' said Ennis. 'I'll think it over a couple of days. We'll meet again Friday night.'

'But if Hatfield has got Fisher scared, how do you figure to get the two outfits in a rukus?' Haskins asked.

'Fisher's men aren't particularly scared,' Ennis replied. 'They're a salty lot, and no matter what's been said, they still believe it was some of the Gomez bunch drygulched their wagons that night under the cliffs below Sanders. They didn't take kind to those killings, nor to losing that big shipment of

Mexican silver, either. It would take very little to make them cut loose. Now forget it and give me time to think. Friday night, right after dark.' With a nod he limped out.

As soon as the door closed behind Ennis, a babble of talk burst forth.

'Well, Clem, what do you think?' asked a scar-faced man. The others hushed to hear what Haskins had to say.

'I don't know,' the sardonic storekeeper admitted. 'He's smart. It ain't often an owlhoot figures a way to make the Texas Rangers work for him. The only thing that bothers me is that maybe some day he'll bite off more than he can chew. But as I said, he's smart. He's built up the tightest organization this section ever knew. And he's pulled us out of some tight spots. I'm backing him to the hilt, but just the same sometimes I worry. If what he's got planned works out, we'll all end up on easy street, but if there's a slip—'

'Then we'll likely end up leaning against passing lead or dancing on nothing,' the other predicted morosely. 'Things ain't been going so good of late.'

'Oh, I don't know,' differed Haskins. 'We made some nice hauls during the past few weeks. That stage job, and Fisher's silver. Adds up to a tidy sum. We're getting together a nice kitty to split when the time comes.'

'If things keep on the way they've been going of late, there won't be many of us left to split it,' the scar-faced man growled.

'One advantage to that, Tobe,' Haskins grinned. 'The fewer to split, the bigger the split.'

'You're right about that,' Tobe agreed, 'if a feller knows for sure he's going to be there at the time.'

'I don't see why we have to wait so long for a split,' another man grumbled querulously. 'Us fellers have earned our share.'

'Jasper,' said Haskins, 'that's where you show how you and Steve are different. He's got brains, you ain't. You know what he says, that many a good bunch has got busted up because of too much money to spend. When some jigger who's never had a dime all of a sudden starts swallerforkin' all over seven counties, folks are going to say, "Where in blazes does he get it?" And somebody is going to make it his business to find out. That's one reason why Steve wants to get control of the legitimate freighting business. Then everybody can see we're making money and nobody will think anything of it when we spend money.'

'He's right, Jasper,' nodded Tobe. 'You just let Steve do the thinking for this bunch and we'll come out on top of the heap.'

'I reckon you're right,' Jasper admitted grudgingly. 'Anyhow, I ain't arguing with anything Ennis says. It ain't healthy. Just the same I ain't going to feel right so long as that damn Hatfield is browsing around and sticking his nose into things. That hellion gives me the creeps. What I wish is somehow Ennis could get into a legitimate rukus with him. Then he'd be taken care of. I don't believe there's a man in all Texas can shade Ennis on the draw.'

Haskins nodded thoughtfully. 'Steve may have something like that in mind,' he observed. 'He's cooking up a scheme to get rid of that rattlesnake, and don't you forget it. Well, I'm going to close this shebang. What are you fellers going to do?'

'Circulate around and have a few drinks, I reckon,' replied Tobe.

'Okay,' Haskins said, 'but no loose talking. Loose talking sometimes leads to a tight rope.'

CHAPTER NINETEEN

Jim Hatfield had plenty to think about, not all of it pleasant. He reflected wryly that as a carting train foreman he was doing a pretty good job, but as a Texas Ranger assigned the chore of cleaning up a lawless element he was, so far, not a particularly outstanding success. True, he had eliminated six of the outlaws. Rather, seven, for he was pretty well satisfied that the dealer, Joe Dawson, had been planted in Kane Fisher's outfit by the outlaw bunch to obtain wanted information and to egg Fisher on in his campaign against the Gomez outfit.

All this was something, all right, and in the tradition of peace officers breaking up lawless organizations. The Curly Bill Brocius gang in Arizona, the Guldens of New Mexico, and the Sam Bass and John Wesley Hardin outfits of Texas had all finally been put out of business by the six-shooter used frequently and effectively.

So far, so good, but the brains of the Javelina bunch was still running loose and so long as the man who boasted the bizarre appellation was free to operate, there would be no peace in the section. Javelina had lost some of his men, but he could easily replace them. There were always plenty of straight-shooting, snake-blooded individuals in the Border country ready to follow any leader who could promise them loot. An outlaw of Javelina's reputation would attract the boldest and most dependable. He could take his pick.

Hatfield was convinced that Steve Ennis was Javelina, but he was forced to admit that all he had to go on was suspicion. There was not one iota of proof against Ennis. Even the title was absurd when applied to him. Javelina! It immediately called to mind a swashbuckling Border raider riding at the head of a pack of bewhiskered objectionables. The antithesis of the suave, polished, eminently correct Ennis.

Ennis was in fact, Hatfield felt, the John Ringo type of outlaw,—cold, calculating, daring and utterly ruthless. And even more

166

dangerous because he had what Ringo had lacked—ambition. Indeed a worthy opponent for the Lone Wolf. A fact Hatfield admitted but did not in the least appreciate. Having a chore to do that had to be done, he would have preferred a less formidable adversary. However, it was impossible for him to dictate just what brand of outlaw he would be up against so he would have to make the best of what circumstances provided.

It would be several days before the train south to Presidio would be ready to roll. Hatfield had another talk with his employer.

'I'm going to ride up to Sanders and look over the railroad situation,' he told Gomez. 'Might be able to pick up a little extra business freighting in supplies.'

Gomez, who was coming to lean more and more on the advice of his cart foreman, raised no objections. Pat wanted to go along, but Hatfield smilingly forbade it.

'Be too busy to look after you,' he said. 'You stay put till I get back.'

'I suppose you'll always be this way,' she pouted. 'You're a regular tomcat—always on the prowl.' Hatfield chuckled and rode north.

'What we're really going to do,' he confided to Goldy, 'is try and locate that cabin where I came so close to getting my come-uppance. I've a notion it's their hangout and if we can find the shack we might turn up something of interest. I don't think my escaping that night

167

would cause them to abandon it. Unless they know I'm a peace officer, and I don't think they do, it would be logical to assume I'd give the place a wide berth, even if I'd figured where it is. I'm pretty sure the trail by which I got back to town runs past it, although I haven't the faintest idea where they turned off that night. And what that lanky jigger said about being back with the Boss within a couple of hours leads me to believe it isn't so very far from Sanders. Anyhow, horse, we're going to have a look-see.'

Hatfield did not think it wise to enter Sanders. No telling who might be hanging around, and the less attention he attracted to himself the better. He turned west a little before sighting the town and rode until he was near the lower slopes of the hills. He turned north and rode along their base until landmarks he had marked told him he was nearing the narrow track that wound upward into their jumbled wilderness. Finally he hit on it and again rode west. He rode with the greatest caution, not knowing what might be ahead. And as he rode he narrowly scanned the slopes to his left. He recalled that when the outlaws turned from the track, they turned left. He slowed Goldy's pace and searched the unbroken line of growth with keen eyes. The turning point must be somewhere within the next mile or so, he felt.

The slope had leveled off and the brush

grew taller and thicker. It was like trying to find a particular tick on a sheep's back to locate the narrow opening that led to the concealed cabin, but eventually he found it.

There wasn't much to mark the spot. Only a slight thinning of the chaparral and an overturned boulder scarred by a horse's iron, but enough for the Lone Wolf. Closer examination discovered broken twigs and scuffed branches where horses had forced their way in.

To ride crashing through the brush would be sheer idiocy. If somebody happened to be in the cabin he would announce his approach a hundred yards away. He rode on for a short distance and turned into the growth. In a little open space where sparse grass grew, he left Goldy and retraced his steps on foot. With the utmost caution he wormed his way through the brush, which quickly thinned, and after about five minutes of slow progress sighted the cabin.

It stood almost concealed by tall chaparral. No sound or movement was apparent. To all appearances it was deserted. He watched for several minutes then took a chance and glided across the open space.

It was breath-catching work and the few steps seemed to take a very long time. Finally he flattened himself against the wall beside the door. A moment of listening and he reached out and gave the door a hard shove. It swung open, banging against the wall. No other sound came from within the building. He hesitated, then, hands on his guns, stepped boldly through the door. The late morning sunshine streaming through the single dusty window showed the cabin without tenancy.

Closing the door, he proceeded to give the place a careful going-over, peering under the bunks, poking the shuck mattresses and tumbled blankets, examining the contents of the shelves, and finding nothing of any significance. It was undoubtedly the gang's hole-up, but it appeared they didn't leave anything around that would more than casually interest a chance visitor.

As a last resort he climbed the rude ladder to the attic-room under the eaves, which was too low to permit him to stand erect. Light filtering through wide cracks between the rough floor boards showed nothing but a number of sacks of oats, evidently feed for the horses. He was about to turn away when an idea struck him. Several of the sacks were open. He thrust his hand into one and probed about. His fingers struck against something hard.

With considerable difficulty he managed to haul the object out from under the covering of oats. It was astonishingly heavy for its size—a whitish metal ingot that must have weighed all of fifty pounds. He instantly catalogued it as a silver brick with a very high gold content, undoubtedly a product of the Clayton Mine.

The sack produced four bricks in all. He placed them on the floor and examined the other sacks.

All but two contained feed, but these two, under a layer of oats, were crammed with silver dollars. He had discovered the outlaws' cache. Pondering what to do about it, he descended the ladder for a look. He turned toward the door and abruptly froze motionless, his head cocked in an attitude of listening. From beyond the closed door came a sharp clicking sound—the beat of horses' irons on the hard ground.

Hatfield glanced swiftly around the room. There was only the one door. The window was barred on the outside with stout wooden strips. He was trapped. The beat of hoofs was swiftly drawing nearer. His hands dropped to the butts of his guns. Looked like he'd have to try to shoot his way out. Then he thought of the room above. There was a chance nobody would go there. He went up the ladder like a cat and even as the horses paused outside, he stretched out on the boards, his eye glued to a crack that gave him a fair view of the room below.

The door opened and two men entered. Hatfield instantly recognized one as the tall member of the trio that brought him to the cabin the night he was attacked on the station steps. The other, a broad, powerfully built individual, he had not seen before.

'Okay, Jasper,' said the tall man, 'get a fire going and make some coffee and fry some bacon. The others'll be here any minute and we can all stand a snack.'

'Shall I feed the horses?' Jasper asked. 'I'll get some oats.' He turned toward the ladder and Hatfield held his breath.

'No,' the other decided. 'Let 'em go light-bellied. We might have some fast travelling to do before the day's over, and a full horse don't run so good. A little grass and water'll hold 'em. I'll take care of it while you make a fire.'

'Okay, Barnes,' Jasper replied and busied himself about the stove. Hatfield relaxed and let out the breath he had been holding.

Barnes came back a little later, sat down and rolled a cigarette. He was still smoking when again hoof beats sounded.

'There they come,' he remarked. 'Hope everything is lined up right.'

Four more men came in. One was Steve Ennis. Hatfield did not know the others.

Ennis walked to a chair and sat down. His leg wound was evidently healing.

'Well, everything is set to go,' he said as he rolled a cigarette.

'The wagon left the mine?' Barnes asked.

'Yes. Rolled right away without any attempt at concealment, and it's loaded for bear. Steel plates bolted to the sides that men can squat behind, with loopholes to shoot through. Six guards inside that wagon. Guess they figure they can beat off any attack. Reckon they could. But if Haskins and the boys handle their end of the chore right their protection won't do them any good. We'll hit them just inside Wild Horse Canyon. It's narrow there, just room enough for the trail, and the slopes are steep. Haskins will wait at the mouth of the canyon, where he can see the trail for a long ways. When they show he'll hightail back up the canyon and get set. We'll be waiting for them.'

'Hope there ain't any slips,' growled Jasper, banging a skillet.

'There won't be,' Ennis replied confidently. 'I've got things planned to the last detail. They'll never know what hit them. We'll make a clean sweep. And with things nicely arranged for Gomez and Fisher, we'll soon be sitting on top of the heap.'

'Hope so,' grunted the pessimistic Jasper. 'Things ain't been going right of late.'

'Oh, stop your croaking!' Ennis exclaimed impatiently.

Jasper growled under his breath but had nothing more to say.

While the outlaws ate and talked, Hatfield listened intently, hoping they would divulge some details of their mysterious plan to rob the treasure wagon. They didn't. But he did pick up another bit of interesting information that corroborated his theory relative to their activities.

'We'll do some more business down around the Border next week,' Ennis said. 'I got word there's some good stuff coming up from Santa Rosalee. We should make a nice haul for Haskins to dispose of. Well, I guess we'd better be moving. That shebang should hit the canyon a couple of hours before sundown.'

He paused, his pale eyes thoughtful. 'Jasper, you stick around the shack,' he ordered. 'Five of us will be enough to handle the chore and I'm getting leary of leaving this place unguarded. If somebody should come snooping around and stumble onto something, it might cost us a pretty penny.'

He glanced at the ladder as he spoke and Hatfield tensed again.

'Okay,' Jasper grunted. 'I'll keep my eyes open. Good huntin'!'

'Let's go,' Ennis said, standing up. With Barnes and the others he left the cabin. Hoofs clicked, fading away into the distance. Hatfield pondered the complication he was suddenly up against. He was determined to reach Wild Horse Canyon before the attempt on the wagon was made, but how the hell to get out of the cabin with Jasper on the ground floor?

He considered winging the hellion with a bullet, through the crack in the floor; but the crack was narrow and the angle bad. He might miss, or he might drill Jasper dead center, which would be uncomfortably like a cold-blooded killing. He decided to wait a little and

174

see what course events would take. Jasper might leave the cabin to fetch water or look after his horse.

But Jasper didn't do any such thing. He puttered about the stove, stacked the dishes and finally sat down with a satisfied grunt. From where he lay, Hatfield could just see his broad back, which was toward the ladder. The odor of burning tobacco drifted upward. A little later Jasper's arm moved as he pinched out the butt. He slumped a little in his chair. Hatfield waited as the minutes ticked by slowly. Jasper was breathing heavily, his head drooped. There was a prolonged snort, then a gentle rumble which Hatfield identified as a snore.

Careful not to make the slightest sound, Hatfield inched toward the open trapdoor. Inch by cautious inch, pausing when Jasper's snore lightened, stealing forward again when it deepened. He reached the opening, slowly and gently lowered his legs through it till his feet rested on one of the rungs. Gripping the edges of the opening he began the descent. And the next rung creaked loudly!

Jasper jerked his head around at the sound. His eyes nearly popped from their sockets. And as he sat paralyzed with astonishment, Hatfield dove at him.

Over went chair and table. Most of the breath was driven from Hatfield's lungs by the force of the impact, but he got a grip on

Jasper's throat and whirled him over on his back.

Taken by surprise though he was, Jasper fought like a madman, and his strength was great. He launched a blow that landed on Hatfield's jaw and blazed fiery light before his eyes. He grabbed for Jasper's gun hand, caught it. They rolled over and over, hitting, kicking, kneeing. Hatfield jolted Jasper's chin with an upward jerk of his wrist and took a stunning return blow between the eyes. Jasper got to his knees beside the overturned table, Hatfield still gripping his throat. With a mighty effort Jasper tore free and staggered to his feet. His hand streaked to his gun.

Prone on the floor, Jim Hatfield drew and shot from the hip. Jasper's gun exploded at the same instant and the Lone Wolf was slammed back by the impact of the slug nicking his shoulder. He fired again and again. With a scream, Jasper whirled around, staggered and crumpled to the floor. Hatfield, gasping and panting, scrambled erect, his thumb hooked over the hammer of his cocked gun. But there was no need for another shot. Jasper was dead, his chest riddled by the slugs from the Ranger's Colt.

CHAPTER TWENTY

Hatfield clung to the leg of the overturned table and pumped some breath back into his lungs. He reloaded his gun and holstered it. He felt sore and bruised all over and the slight cut in the flesh of his shoulder smarted, but his strength quickly returned.

There was warm coffee in the pot on the stove. Hatfield poured a cup, swallowed at a gulp and followed it with another. Then he wiped his lips and glanced around the room. What to do next?

He pondered a moment, then climbed the ladder to the attic. He stuffed the gold bricks into the sack and dropped it to the floor below. Climbing down, he retrieved the sack and shouldered it, grunting with the weight. The silver dollars he decided to leave behind. They were too bulky and would take too much time to move. He carried the sack into the brush and carefully concealed it, marking the spot well. Then he returned to the cabin and packed Jasper's heavy body into the brush, covering it with twigs and leaves and dead branches.

'Now when and if those hellions come back and find Jasper gone and the gold missing, they'll very likely figure he did a little stealing on his own and trailed his twine. Hope so, anyhow.'

He entered the cabin again and straightened things up, righting the overturned chair and table and removing all signs of the battle. There were some blood stains on the floor, but he didn't think they would be noticed among the numerous grease spots and other dirt.

Without difficulty he caught the outlaw's horse, which was grazing nearby, mounted it and rode to where he left Goldy. He switched to the big sorrel, leading the other cayuse by the bridle, and rode swiftly down the trail. When he reached the Chihuahua he turned south. A mile farther on he halted, removed the rig from the led horse and tossed it into the brush, turning the animal loose to fend for itself, which he knew it was capable of doing. Then he rode on until he reached the last bend in the trail north of Wild Horse Canyon. He turned west and rode parallel to the northern slope of the hills that hemmed the canyon. It would not do to enter the gorge. Not until he was some distance from its mouth and screened by thickets and groves did he turn south again. Then he sent Goldy up the long slope until he was not far below the rimrock.

It was a hard pull and the sorrel was blowing badly when they reached a point where it was possible to ride parallel to the gorge floor, but nearly a thousand yards above it. Hatfield let Goldy rest for a few minutes and then started on again. He knew he could not be seen from the canyon floor so long as he hugged the rimrock. He got the best speed possible from his mount, anxiously straining his ears for sounds that would indicate trouble below. The sun was low in the west and Ennis had said that the wagon would reach the canyon a couple of hours before it set. It was with a sigh of relief that he saw the cliffs where the hills petered out to the south.

'Have to leave you again for a while, feller,' he told Goldy as he removed the bit and loosened the cinches. 'Take it easy now till I come back.'

Drawing his Winchester from the saddle boot, he began to work his way down the sag toward the canyon floor.

The going was slow, for the sound of a rolling stone would travel a long ways in the hush of evening. He slowed still more as he descended farther and knew he couldn't risk a much nearer approach. Finally he reached a point from which he could see the canyon mouth and a few hundred yards into its depths to where it began to bend. He could also see for a considerable distance along the broad Chihuahua Trail rolling up from the south.

Just inside the canyon mouth a man sat a horse and peered along the trail. Hatfield could not make out his features but assumed he must be Clem Haskins. His attitude was one of tense expectancy.

Slowly the minutes crawled past and Haskins, if it was Haskins, made no move. Hatfield wondered where the others were holed up. On the opposite slope, perhaps. He felt pretty sure they couldn't see him, but just the same there was an uncertainty that was hard on the nerves. Not pleasant to ponder the possibility that a rifle barrel might at the moment be lined in his direction.

However, nothing happened. The silence remained undisturbed. Nothing moved and there was no sign of life save the motionless horseman in the gorge mouth. How in the devil did they figure to work it, Hatfield wondered. He searched the slopes and what he could see of the canyon for the answer, and found none.

Suddenly the horseman straightened in his saddle, head thrust forward. Then he whirled his mount and rode swiftly up the canyon. Gazing along the gray ribbon of the trail, Hatfield saw a big freight wagon come into sight. It was drawn by six sturdy horses and was moving fast.

'Well, we'll know what's what in a few more minutes.' he muttered, cocking his rifle.

On came the wagon. Now Hatfield could faintly hear the grind of the tires and the click of the horses' irons. He could make out the driver perched on his high seat, which appeared to be singularly cooped in, doubtless by the same protection the high sides provided for the guards crouched in the bed. The wagon did look about as impregnable as such a vehicle could be made.

The equipage reached the canyon mouth, rolled in between the encroaching slopes. And Hatfield suddenly heard a low mutter of sound that quickly increased to a thudding roar interspersed by a wild bleating and bellowing.

'Well, I'll be damned!' he exclaimed, flinging the rifle to his shoulder and holding it rock-steady.

Around the bend poured a sea of tossing shaggy heads, clashing horns and rolling eyes that filled the gorge from side to side. It was a herd of cattle in mad stampede.

Head on the stampede hit the wagon, tons of frenzied flesh and bone. The horses tried wildly to turn and flee. The wheels cramped, the wagon went over, the horses fell. Cows piled up on top of the howling mess. The stampede split, the outer cattle being hurled into the brush, to scramble out again beyond the mad tangle and go charging down the gorge.

And from the growth of the opposite slope swarmed half a dozen men, guns blazing.

Hatfield glanced along the sights. Through the spurtle of smoke he saw one of the outlaws crumple up. He fired again and a second pitched forward on his face. The others dived wildly for cover, Hatfield speeding them with bullets. He shifted the rifle muzzle as four horsemen came bulging around the bend after the herd they had stampeded, yelling and shooting. One spun from his saddle as the Winchester spoke. The others jerked their mounts to a halt, giving Hatfield a fair target. Another instant and four horses were speeding back around the bend, two of them riderless.

Hatfield swung the rifle around and raked the brush with slugs till the magazine was empty. Some of the guards, evidently not seriously hurt, were also shooting into the brush. As he stuffed fresh cartridges into the magazine, Hatfield reflected it must be rather warm for anybody who happened to still be there.

Tucking the rifle under his arm, he began working down the slope. Before he left cover he raised his voice in a shout—

'Hold it, down there, I'm coming out!'

The firing ceased. He stepped from the brush to face a bristle of gun barrels. He walked forward unconcernedly, the rifle still tucked under his arm. The guards stared at him.

'Feller,' one of them called, 'I don't know who the hell you are or where the hell you came from, but you sure saved our bacon. *Gracias, Amigo!* as the oilers say.'

'Anybody badly hurt?' Hatfield asked.

'Oh, we're all cut and scratched and bruised and gourged, and I'm scairt Tim's got a busted arm,' the other replied. 'Nobody killed, though. You chased the sidewinders off before they really got going good. Got yourself some of 'em, too. That pair over by the brush ain't moved, and I think the two up ahead got their come-uppance, too.'

The wagon driver limped up. 'One horse got a busted neck, poor devil!' he announced, 'and we'll have to shoot the off leader. He's all smashed to pieces.'

While the horses were being loosed from the tangled harness and gotten onto their feet, Hatfield examined the bodies of the dead outlaws. One of the pair by the brush was the lanky Barnes, the other had entered the cabin with Ennis. The two farther up the canyon he did not recall seeing before.

'But the big he-wolf of the pack slipped out of the loop,' he growled. 'Well, I've got a pretty good case started against him now; a little more and I'll have it cinched. I'll need more, though. The way things stand, unless one of his hellions could be induced to talk, I wouldn't dare take him to court. It would be man against man, with such angles as mistaken identity, personal ambition or animosity on my part and hell knows what else brought into the picture. A smart lawyer would be able to make my charge look a bit flimsy, and there's never any telling what a jury is liable to do. The horned toad has build up an excellent reputation in the section and that would have to be overcome. No, I can't risk it. I've either

183

got to tie onto something more definite or maneuver him into a position where he'll tip his own hand. Fact is, I don't think he'll ever come to court. He's not that sort. At the showdown he's very likely to go out in a blaze of glory. Well, that's all right. The old saying is that the only good outlaw is a dead one, and there's considerable truth in it. Lock 'em up for a spell and when they get out, they all too often start over where they left off, and innocent folks suffer in consequence. Well, we'll see.'

He went back to the wagon. 'Did you fellows recognize any of those that got away?' he asked hopefully. There was a general shaking of heads.

'Guess we were too busy trying to get out of the tangle to pay much attention,' said the driver, 'and unless I'm a lot mistaken, they had neckerchiefs pulled up over their faces.'

Hatfield nodded; he expected as much. 'Well, let's see if we can't get that wagon back on its wheels,' he suggested. 'Doesn't appear to be damaged much. I've a notion the running gear is in working order.'

After considerable effort to the accompaniment of much profanity, they finally got the wagon righted. While the broken harness was being patched up, Hatfield went to the edge of the brush and whistled a long note. From far up the slope came an answering whinny and a crackling in the growth as Goldy made his way down to his master.

While waiting for him, Hatfield pondered the situation and what he should do next. The fleeing outlaws might make for the cabin in the hills and they might not. Either way he couldn't very well set out in pursuit. He was not in very good shape and his horse was tired. And the odds were a bit too heavy. Also, night was not far off and it was doubtful if he could find the shack in the dark. He decided it was best to trail along to Sanders with the wagon.

He craved something to eat, a drink and bed. Tomorrow was another day.

The battered horses were hitched to the wagon and the sadly mauled equipage got under way again. The bodies of the slain outlaws were left where they lay.

'Let the sheriff pick 'em up and add them to his collection,' Hatfield said. 'He's going to be fit to be tied when he hears about this, but I don't reckon he can do much about it.'

It was long after dark when the wagon limped into Sanders. Hatfield stabled his weary horse, gave him a good rubdown and made sure all his wants were provided for. Then he repaired to the Cattleman's Hotel restaurant for a much needed meal.

Seated at a table was the sardonic Clem Haskins, calmly eating his dinner. Without batting an eyelash he nodded a greeting to Hatfield and went on eating.

'Talk about cold nerve!' the Ranger

muttered as he sat down at another table. 'That sidewinder would rake in the pot on a busted flush against a full-house!'

CHAPTER TWENTY-ONE

Sanders buzzed over the frustrated attempt to rob the treasure wagon. Prominent citizens sought out Hatfield to congratulate him on the part he played in the affair.

'You ought to be sheriff of this county,' one declared. 'Stick around, son, and we'll elect you next year, sure as shootin'!' Others nodded sober agreement.

All of which was pleasant but did not help solve Hatfield's problem.

'Well, many a pot has been won by a bluff,' he told himself. 'Maybe the hellions will slip and give me a chance to run one.'

The following morning Hatfield visited the construction superintendent of the railroad project.

'Glad you dropped in,' the super said after Hatfield introduced himself. 'We can use some freighting service. Down to the southwest, not far, is a good stand of live oak that will make fine crossties, but the man who owns the grove hasn't adequate carting facilities. And there are other things you can handle for us. I've been dickering a bit with that fellow Haskins who owns a store here, but yesterday I received a letter from Mr. Dunn directing me to negotiate with your outfit.'

They talked over details for a while and tentative contracts were drawn up.

'I'll have Gomez ride up and sign,' Hatfield promised. 'I'm sure he'll be satisfied with the terms you offer and you'll find him a nice person to deal with.'

After his talk with the super, Hatfield saddled Goldy and headed back to Aguilar. He felt there was nothing to be gained from hanging around Sanders any longer.

He rode through the sinister canyon, where the stark forms of the dead outlaws still lay. The sheriff had been notified and would take care of them. Hatfield chuckled as he thought of what the crusty old peace officer's reaction must have been to the report.

'Reckon he's more than ever convinced I'm a bad luck piece,' he told Goldy.

Riding warily but swiftly he covered the distance in good time and with no mishap. He decided not to go on to Aguilar and when he reached the track that led to the Clover Leaf ranchhouse he turned into it.

Pat was sitting on the porch when he rode up. She ran to meet him and looked him over.

'So!' she said accusingly, 'been mixed up in something else, I see. You've got a blue eye and a hole in your shirt. I suppose there's a hole in your shoulder, too. Come on in and let me take care of it. You might as well show it to me right now.'

Inside the ranchhouse she made him strip off his shirt. She was treating the slight wound when Gomez entered.

'You'll be the death of all of us yet,' he declared resignedly. 'Now what happened?'

Hatfield told them of the attack on the treasure wagon, omitting the preliminary details.

'I happened along at just the right time and figured I'd better take a hand,' he concluded.

Pat looked skeptical but didn't question him.

Gomez was pleased with the news relating to the railroad contracts. 'I'll ride up there tomorrow or the day after,' he said. 'Now there's no sense in you going to Aguilar today. Everything is running smoothly and the train for Presidio isn't ready yet. You deserve a little rest after all you've gone through.'

Hatfield didn't argue the point. He felt he could steal a chance to take it easy for a spell.

After a leisurely breakfast the following morning, he got the rig on Goldy and was preparing to depart when a horseman came speeding up the trail on a lathered and blowing cayuse. It was old Si Perkins. His eyes were wild and he breathed in hoarse gasps.

'Jim!' he gulped as he dropped to the ground. 'Thank Pete I found you here! All blazes is busting loose in town. They found

Kane Fisher dead this morning, right outside our station, a knife in his back. His men are making big medicine. They're in the Last Chance getting likkered up and swear they're going to clean out the Gomez outfit. Our boys are holed up in the station and daring 'em to do it. Fisher's bunch aim to get behind that corral wall across the street and burn the station and shoot it out. Things are liable to cut loose any minute.'

Hatfield turned to Gomez. 'Looks like it's showdown,' he said quietly. 'Have you got a double-barrelled shotgun and some buckshot shells? Right! Get them. And have a horse saddled for Perkins, the best in your stables.'

While Pat ran upstairs to get the scattergun, Gomez bellowed orders to his wranglers. Hatfield was meanwhile fumbling with a cunningly concealed secret pocket in his broad leather belt. He pinned something to his shirt front.

'Madre de Dios!' exclaimed Gomez, staring at the gleaming silver star set on a silver circle, the feared and honored badge of the Texas Rangers.

'And, feller, I got you placed at last!' whooped Perkins. 'I been puzzling over you for quite a spell, and now I've got you placed. Gentlemen, hush!'

'Yes, I'm a Ranger,' Hatfield told Gomez. 'Captain McDowell sent me here to find out what was going on and try and clean up the mess. I've found out. Next in order is the clean-up, if those loco carters don't tangle the twine!'

Pat appeared with the shotgun. Her eyes widened a little as she gazed at the Ranger star, but she did not appear particularly surprised.

'Thought so, ever since that night at—at Sanders.'

'Is Steve Ennis in town?' Hatfield asked Perkins as he tightened his cinches.

'Sure,' Perkins replied. 'He's at the Last Chance. That ice-nerved Clem Haskins is with him. Haskins has been setting up the drinks, and I think he's egging on the Fisher bunch.'

'Quite likely,' Hatfield agreed grimly. 'Where the devil is the sheriff?'

'He got a call to go over to Marathon,' Perkins answered. 'Took his two deputies with him.'

Hatfield nodded, and wondered how authentic the call was.

A wrangler came hurrying from the stable, leading a magnificent black horse, saddled and bridled.

'He's never been beaten in a race,' Gomez said pridefully.

Hatfield smiled a little and swung into the saddle.

'Be seeing you,' he said. 'Trail, Goldy, Trail!'

The great sorrel shot forward. A few

minutes later Gomez swore incredulously.

'I would have wagered all I own that there wasn't a horse in all Texas could show heels to Diablo, but that yellow demon is drawing away from him.'

Hatfield settled himself in the saddle and gave his whole attention to getting everything from the speeding sorrel. The trail flowed under Goldy's drumming irons. Trees lining the road rushed to meet them, sailed away to the rear. Goldy had gotten his second wind and his speed increased. His flashing hoofs kicked up clouds of dust, but Hatfield rode in clear air. He glanced over his shoulder and saw the great black was steadily falling behind.

'Go to it, feller!' he chuckled. 'You're already five feet ahead of your shadow!'

Goldy snorted, rolled his eyes, flattened his ears and slugged his head above the bit. With effortless ease he fairly poured his long body over the ground.

As landmarks came into view and flashed past, Hatfield estimated the distance yet to go. The minutes ticked off, altogether too swiftly. Hatfield knew that every second could be vital. Perkins hadn't exaggerated the seriousness of the danger. The long expected explosion had come at last and a cart war had erupted that could make the desperate battle at Goliad look mild. Even now the situation might be completely out of hand.

Far ahead showed the buildings of Aguilar,

looking like doll houses in the distance, and a few minutes later Hatfield heard, above the pound of Goldy's hoofs, a snapping and crackling as of thorns burning under a pot, increasing quickly to a stutter of gunfire. The ball had opened!

Hatfield knew that coming in from the north he would be to the rear of the low stone wall behind which Perkins said Fisher's carters would hole up. A little later he slowed Goldy's pace and allowed the outraged black to come abreast of him.

'I aim to get behind them,' he told Perkins. 'If I can get close enough before they spot me, I think I can control them. If I can't, and you figure to be in this with me, shoot fast and try to stay alive, which will be considerable of a chore.'

'I'm with you,' Perkins declared sturdily. 'If it comes to a showdown we'll go out together, and send a few to open Hell Gates for us.'

'Okay,' Hatfield replied, 'but don't make a move till I do. Now if we can just get close.'

'We can work it,' Perkins said confidently. 'There's an open space behind that wall, with a flock of shacks and dobes fronting it. We can slip between them and be right on top of the hellions before they know it. They'll be all looking to the front, anyhow.'

When Perkins gave the word they dismounted and made their way through the narrow opening between two adobe huts.

'Listen to those guns crack!' breathed Perkins. 'They're sure using up ammunition. Look, there they are!'

Hatfield peered ahead and saw, less than forty yards distant, a line of figures crouched behind the rough stone wall, across the street from which loomed the sprawling station building. Smoke billowed upward as guns cracked intermittently. From the station came answering shots that thudded against the wall or screeched over it. Even as he gazed, a ball of flaming oil-soaked rags sailed through the air, thudded against the station wall and dropped to the ground. The distance was a bit great for accurate throwing.

'But if one lands on those dry shingles, the whole shebang will go up in minutes. You stay here,' he told Perkins, and strode forward into the open, the shotgun held waist high.

So engrossed with what was in front of them, the bunch behind the wall never noted his approach until he was less than a score of feet distant. Then his voice rolled forth in thunder.

'Hold it! In the name of the State of Texas! Drop those guns, disperse and go about your business in an orderly manner! This is an unlawful gathering!'

The carters whirled, guns ready; then they 'froze' staring at the grim figure fronting them. Hatfield's face was bleak as chiseled granite, his eyes the color of frosted steel. The twin muzzles of the shotgun yawned hungrily, and on his broad breast gleamed the star of the Rangers.

'Hold it!' he repeated. 'Don't make a move. This thing packs eleven buckshot to the barrel and it'll spray you like a hose! I'll kill the first man who makes a move, and a dozen more along with him!'

'God a'mighty!' a hoarse voice shouted. 'That feller's a Ranger!'

'Yeah!' bawled old Perkins. 'He's a Ranger, and—the Lone Wolf! Ever hear of him, boys?'

They had. Jaws dropped, men stared open-mouthed at the legendary figure whose exploits were the talk of the whole Southwest.

The carters were bold and reckless men, their passions fired by alcohol and anger, and fronting them was a single man. They could kill him—they were fifty to one—a single shot would do it. But before he fell those black muzzles would flame. And how many would go down before their lethal blast? Each man had a crawling apprehension that he was one of those singled out. They hesitated, fingering their weapons.

Hatfield spoke again, his voice quiet. 'I'm giving you one more chance,' he said. 'You are defying law and order.' His voice blared at them— 'Drop those guns!' The hammers of the shotgun clicked back to full cock.

A voice bawled a protest: 'Hold it, feller, we ain't fighting no Rangers, but if we let go our irons those buzzards across the street will murder us.'

'No they won't,' Hatfield replied. 'I'll take care of them. Drop your guns.'

There was a clatter and thud as hardware fell to the ground. Hatfield beckoned to Perkins and tossed him the shotgun. He walked forward and looked the huddled group up and down. Then he proceeded to give them such a tongue-lashing as never a bunch of shame-faced desperadoes got before.

'You're acting like a bunch of hooched-up Comanches,' he concluded. 'Just as terrapin-brained. I'm telling you, the Gomez outfit didn't kill Kane Fisher, and they didn't drygulch your wagons. Both outfits have been duped by a smart owlhoot who played you against each other, and you fell for it. Stay put till I come back.'

He vaulted the wall and crossed the street to the suddenly silent station.

'Miguel! Felipe!' he called, 'Come out of there, and bring everybody with you, and leave your guns behind.'

There was a mutter of talk inside the building, then the door opened and the Gomez carters filed out. Hatfield led them around the wall and lined them up beside the others. 'Now I've had enough foolishness from all of you,' he told them. 'I want you to get together, understand one another and behave yourselves as good Texans should.' He turned

195

to the Fisher men.

'The chances are you fellows will all be working for Gomez before long, and glad to do it,' he said. 'What's past is forgotten, so far as I'm concerned. It'll never be brought up unless you do something to make me bring it up.'

He turned his back on the sheepish carters who had suddenly forgotten all about wanting to kill one another, and walked away.

'Si,' he said to Perkins, 'sometimes a good bluff will take the pot. I believe this is one of the times.'

'Where you headed for, Jim?' Perkins asked anxiously.

'The Last Chance,' Hatfield replied. 'And keep behind me when we go in.'

People who had been watching the battle from advantageous spots were crowding the street. They stared at the tall Ranger, but the look on his face kept them from speaking to him.

Reaching the Last Chance, Hatfield pushed through the swinging doors and glanced about. At the far end of the bar stood Steve Ennis and Clem Haskins. Ennis wet his lips with his tongue as Hatfield walked toward him. Haskins glowered, the veins at his temples swelling like cords. Hatfield halted a dozen paces distant from the pair. He spoke, his voice quiet but carrying throughout the room, 'In the name of the State of Texas I arrest

Steve Ennis and Clem Haskins for the murder of Kane Fisher and for conspiracy to commit murder. Anything you say—'

With a wordless howl, Haskins jerked his gun. Ennis dived into the back room and slammed the door.

Back and forth spurted the lances of flame as Ranger and owlhoot shot it out. A bullet grazed Hatfield's cheek, another twitched his sleeve. Then he lowered his smoking gun and gazed down at Haskins writhing and moaning on the floor, blood dyeing his shirt front scarlet.

'Keep an eye on him, Si,' Hatfield said and tried the door of the back room. It was locked.

Stepping back he hurled his weight against it. The stout planks groaned and creaked but stood firm. Hatfield tried again, with no better results. He turned and left the saloon, unhurriedly, men making way for him in silence. He walked around the corner of the building and peered up and down the alley. The door leading onto it stood open; nobody was in sight. Hatfield rolled and lighted a cigarette, drawing in deep drags of the soothing smoke.

A man came hurrying up. 'You looking for Ennis, Ranger?' he asked. 'He just rode out of town, headed south.'

'Thanks,' Hatfield replied and re-entered the saloon.

Somebody had summoned a doctor and he

was working over Haskins who was unconscious from shock and loss of blood.

'Hit pretty hard, but I've a notion maybe he'll pull through,' said the doctor. 'What you want done with him?'

'Put him to bed and set a guard over him till the sheriff gets back to town and takes him in charge,' Hatfield directed. He turned to Perkins.

'Si,' he said, 'go look after my horse. Give him a good rubdown, water with a dash of whiskey in it and a helping of oats. I want to get something to eat. I've a notion I'll need it.'

'Okay,' answered Perkins and hurried out to attend to the chore.

Hatfield was eating when Miguel Allende entered, accompanied by a little man with dead looking eyes.

'*Capitan,*' he announced, 'this is Malone, who had charge of the late Senor Fisher's guards. He would like to talk to you.'

'Sit down, Malone.' Hatfield invited. 'What's on your mind?'

Malone dropped into a chair and regarded the Ranger for a moment.

'Hatfield,' he said, 'I ain't much good and haven't been for quite a spell, but somehow when you talked to us over there, I got a feeling that if I had a chance maybe I might be able to pick up where I left off a few years back. Do you think Gomez would take me on?'

'I'm sure he would,' Hatfield replied warmly. 'Fact is, I'll promise you he will.' He reached his hand across the table.

Malone stood up and smiled, with lips, Hatfield felt, that had not smiled for a long time.

'He'll never regret doing it,' he said, his voice a little husky. With a nod he walked out, his head up, his shoulders squared.

'If they've got something worth while in them, better to save them than to shoot them,' the Ranger mused and went on eating.

CHAPTER TWENTY-TWO

By the time Hatfield had finished his meal, Goldy was brought around, looking none the worse for his gruelling drive from the Clover Leaf ranch. Hatfield mounted and rode south on the Chihuahua Trail.

He did not push the horse. He had a fifty-mile ride ahead of him. Ennis would doubtless travel at top speed for a while, but he would have to slow down before long, and Hatfield was confident that Goldy's greater endurance would bring him to Presidio on the heels of the fleeing outlaw.

'I'm gambling that he's headed for Ojinaga,' Hatfield told his horse. 'For Ojinaga and that storekeeper who handled the goods his bunch stole from Mexican cart trains. If he gives us the slip he'll get another bunch together in no time and be right back in business. Once he's across the Rio Grande, he'll figure he's safe, but he won't be.'

The afternoon wore on, a globe of color and fragrance, as Goldy's steady, even pace ate up the miles. The western sky flamed scarlet and gold, softened to rose and violet, paled to steel gray. The rhythmic beat of Goldy's hoofs sounded louder in the hush of twilight. One by one the bonfire stars of Texas blazed overhead. The trail stretched on, a gray ribbon of mystery in the wan light.

It was midnight when Hatfield reached Presidio. He rode to the bank of the Rio Grande and gazed across the dark water to where twinkling lights marked the site of the Mexican town of Ojinaga. For some minutes he sat motionless in his saddle, then he unpinned his Ranger badge and stowed it in the secret pocket.

'Horse,' he said, 'over there I don't pack any more official authority than a rabbit in a houndog's mouth; but I sat in this game and I'll have to play out the hand. So here goes for an International incident.' He headed Goldy across the river.

From Miguel, Hatfield had learned the location of the store in question. He rode through the dark and silent streets until it was but a block distant. He pulled up, hitched

Goldy to a convenient rack and proceeded on foot.

A light burned in the store. Standing by the counter two men talked together. One was a fat Mexican, undoubtedly the owner. The other was Steve Ennis. Hatfield opened the door and walked in.

'Trail's end, Ennis,' he said as the pair turned to face him. 'Coming back to Texas with me?'

Ennis' pale eyes seemed to glaze. He stared unbelievingly at the Ranger.

'You—you have no authority down here and you know it,' he said thickly.

'I'm packing all the authority I need,' Hatfield returned significantly. 'Ennis, you have two choices: come back to Texas and stand trial, or eat lead! Take your pick.'

Ennis seemed to hesitate, then he shrugged his shoulders. 'I don't believe you've got a case against me that would hold water,' he said. 'So I guess I might as well ride back with you.'

He turned as if to speak to the Mexican, whirled and went for his gun.

He was fast, lightning-fast, but Hatfield drew and shot him before he could pull trigger. Ennis sprang into the air, his hands clutching wildly, as if in a vain attempt to grasp his own departing soul, and crashed to the floor.

Hatfield holstered his gun and gazed regretfully at the dead outlaw, a man who might easily have made an outstanding success of life, if he'd only ridden a straight trail. With a sigh he turned to the cowering storekeeper.

'*Amigo,*' he said pleasantly, 'you have been dealing with a notorious killer and *ladrone.* You know it and I know it. I'm going to give you a mite of advice. Get out of business, before the *rurales* hear about it. They won't have much patience with you.'

'I will, Senor, I will,' the other quavered.

'See that you do,' Hatfield said and walked out.

Heads were poking cautiously from windows, there was a murmur of agitated voices in the darkness.

'Senor, what happened?' somebody called.

'A little trouble in the store,' Hatfield answered. 'It's all taken care of.' A moment later he mounted Goldy and rode back across the River.

Hatfield did not pause in Presidio, but continued to ride north for several miles. In a thicket beside a little stream he took the rig off his tired horse and turned him loose to graze. Then, with his saddle for a pillow, he stretched out on the soft grass and was almost instantly asleep.

Late the following afternoon, Hatfield reached Aguilar. His first chore was to look up Sheriff Thomas.

There was a twinkle in the old peace officer's eyes as he shook hands.

202

'Thought you had me fooled, eh?' he chuckled. 'Well you didn't. I knew Bill McDowell before you cut your first teeth, and I know how he works. I spotted you first off, but my chore was to keep quiet and play dumb. Much obliged for cleaning up the mess; it was beyond me. Now maybe I can get some sleep. You had things figured out just right. Haskins thought he was going to die, though I reckon he ain't, and he talked plenty. He killed Fisher and planted his body in front of Gomez' station. Then he and Ennis spread about that Gomez' hands were responsible. They got Fisher's men likkered up and egged them on to shoot it out with the Gomez bunch.'

'Yes, they planned to take over the carting business, for its own worth and because it provided them a perfect outlet for the goods they stole in Mexico,' Hatfield said. 'It's easy to rob trains down there, but not easy to dispose of the stolen goods. They had a nice scheme worked out. That's why they started the trouble between the two outfits in the first place. It was easier because Fisher was dealing in smuggled goods.'

'I don't see how you ever caught on to Ennis,' said the sheriff. 'I'd never have suspected him of wearing a blotted brand. How'd you do it?'

'Largely through a process of elimination,' Hatfield replied. 'I'd discarded about every other suspect. Learning that he was a director of the Clayton Mine and able to learn things about the gold shipments that were robbed helped. He was the only one of the directors who wasn't altogether above suspicion. But he proceeded to make the kind of a slip the owlhoot brand usually makes, sooner or later. When he lied to me up at Sanders about how he got his hurt leg. He didn't need to do that. But when he handed me that yarn about his horse pitching him, he called the thing to my attention. And it was easy to see that he'd recently been shot. That set me to really thinking about him. Learning that he was acquainted with that crooked card dealer I killed the night Gomez' train was drygulched helped, too. Give them time and they always slip. I admit I still didn't have much of a case on him, so I tried a little bluff. I figured Haskins would go off half-cocked when I accused him of the murder of Fisher. He did.

'Incidentally, I'll take you up to that cabin in the hills west of Sanders and you can pack back the gold the Clayton Mine lost in that stage robbery. I've got it nicely cached, along with another body for your collection. Well, I'm riding over to the Clover Leaf to see Gomez and give him the lowdown on things. Then I've got to get back to the Post.'

Gomez was heartbroken at losing his foreman, both for business and personal reasons.

'You have done me a great service,' he

declared. 'I owe you more than I could ever possibly repay. I wish you'd stay here and help me run the business. I'm not as young as I used to be.'

'Right now I've got another job,' Hatfield replied. 'But later, well, you never can tell.'

Two days later he said good-bye to Pat as he sat his horse by the veranda steps.

'You'll be back, Jim?' she asked softly, her eyes misted.

'Yes,' he promised, 'I'll be back. I've got to get over to the Post and see what Captain Bill has lined up, but I'll be back.'

He reached down and lifted her lightly from the ground and held her close for a moment.

'I'll—be—back,' he repeated and rode off, her kiss warm on his lips.